Lost Realms of the 9th Parallel

Posted Gear

Published by Posted Gear, 2024.

LOST REALMS OF THE 9TH PARALLEL

First edition. March 13, 2024.

ISBN: 979-8224389353

Written by Posted Gear.

Table of Contents

Ch1. You find a job yet?

Coffee, Bacon, and a subtle tension fills the air in the Benson household. A house located in the suburbs, on a foothill of Kinsridge. This part of Kinsridge is known to be fairly quiet, just as the Bensons are known to be the same. Of course, with the exception of the Benson's oldest son Brick, who also happens to be the topic of a very mild argument taking place in the kitchen this morning. Brick's parents, Pete and Jackie can't seem to agree on what to do with him now that he has been suspended from school for fighting.

The usual racket overhead in the upstairs bedrooms follows a series of alarms for each of the kids goes off and the kids of the house make their way downstairs for breakfast. Brick has a brother and sister that are identical twins, Zack and Samantha just a year younger than him. The three sit down for breakfast just as they normally do before the kids' bike or skate off to school and Pete heads off to work. Jackie, currently in between jobs, listens to the morning AM radio while cooking breakfast, cleaning, and getting the kids lunches ready as Pete reads the paper and sips his coffee. This morning Jackie has the radio turned down to a faint mumble alongside her while washing dishes.

"Looks like it's still raining," Pete says. "If you kids want a ride to school, you'd better eat and get changed quick.

A few minutes passed, everyone had scarfed down there food fairly quick and just about all get up at the same time and started walking toward to the kitchen sink to set their dishes before heading back upstairs to get ready for school. Pete waited until the kids made it just about up the stairs before saying, "Hold up, Brick."

Brick, who had full intentions hanging out all day and playing games most of the day paused mid step for a moment before heading back down to the kitchen to have a word with his father.

"Your mother and I talked about your little incident at school. I don't know what to tell you, son. Your councilor said you were standing up for you buddy Raj, right?"

"Yea, what was I supposed to do? Let Him get beat up?"

"No...I don't know. Of course not, I probably would have done the same thing. It's just that this isn't the first time, last time you were sticking up for your brother, before that it was for yourself. I Just don't know why you kids are having such a problem at school and I'm not sure why you always have to be the one to jump in to save everybody. They're gunna have to learn to stand up for them self someday. Go ahead and get dressed, you're coming to work with me."

Brick says "Okay," and makes his way upstairs to get ready. As he's putting on his pants, he hears a faint, "ha-ha" through the hallway from Samantha. "You thought you were stayin' home."

Brick turns his head to the doorway, which is directly across the hallway from Zack's room, just to see him with grin on his face. Zack asks if he thinks he is gunna be able to go the bon fire that weekend. "I doubt it," Brick replied, "Remember what happened last time?"

"Yea, you weren't allowed anywhere for a month," Zack said. "Well, Samantha and Kate wanna check out that old Asylum after. The beach closes at 10, we can pick you up on our way there."

"Uhh—yea, I don't know about that one."

"What? Asks Samantha, "are you afraid your gunna fall out the window again?"

Brick lightly replies, "no."

"You sure? She asks. "Because it kinda sounds like your scared."

Brick quickly changes the subject, having just found himself in trouble and recently noticed enough unrelated tension between their parents. He asks about what looks like the inside of an old TV remote with a light slowly pulsing on Zack's desk.

"What's that blinking on your desk?" he asks.

Zack turns to the project covered desk and replies. "Uhh...it's supposed to be a cricket."

"...A cricket?" Brick asks with a confused look.

"Yea, I ran out a Piezos" Said Zack. "I have plenty of lights left over from what I put in your amp though."

Brick, with an even more confused look on his says, "A pie—zo? a what? Ah never mind, let's go." Before calling out to his sister who had stepped into room. "Samantha, you ready?...SAM?"

With no response from Samantha, Brick walks over to her room. He looks in the doorway past the mess of clothes to see her laying on her bed, head below a wall of posters, with her headphones on, reading a book. Brick walks up and lightly slaps Samantha's foot and says, "Let's go, Sam."

They make their way down to the kitchen where Pete is still at the kitchen table with the morning paper. "I take it everyone is ready...alright, let's go." he said, as he folded up the newspaper and they head out to the car.

Kinsridge High, where the kids attend is a few miles from their house. Today Pete decides to take advantage of the few minutes he has with all of the kids together in the car. He nervously glances over at Brick on his right then into the rearview before breaking the cold silence with, "I'm sure you guys have been wondering what is going on with your mother, huh?"

After no response from her brothers Samantha says, "She got laid off, right?"

"Well, yea...but uh...there is a little more going on. Her mother, your grandmother just passed the other night. She didn't know how to tell you. They were never that close and now there is nothing she can do about it. She had always wanted to make things right between them but didn't know how. Your mother has been having a hard time dealing with things right now. I don't know how to help her with that, I'm still trying to figure out how we are going to pay for things now that she's out of work." Pete said.

The sound of wiper blades zipping back and forth along splashing puddles carry on as the kids process things.

Though they did not spend much time in recent years with her, they can recall time spent hiking, camping, and fishing or even shooting once in a great while in the mountains that fell just outside their neighborhood. Being retired and a widow for many years, this was how she kept herself busy. She chose to spend her time with the kids over summer breaks or weekends until their summer school and sports seemed to suddenly replace that time once they got into high school.

They pull up to school and Pete says, "I'm sorry to dump that on you kids first thing in the morning...you do your best to keep your chin up and your head straight. Oh, and Uh-h please be careful getting home, I know you don't have anything to ride. I've been reading about robberies and all sorts of things going on in town lately."

Pete and Brick head north a couple blocks to get on the main highway that runs along the foothills, toward Pete's work on the other side of town. Pete spends most of the car ride lost in thought, he just took on a substantial amount of work and responsibility at work without any additional compensation. He is so bothered by it that he nearly misses his exit.

"Brick, I'm not gunna be able to bring you into my new office" said Pete. "Sorry, we won't get to hang out like we used to.

"You got a new office?" asked Brick.

Pete forgot for a moment that he hadn't got around to sharing the news. "Yea, I didn't tell you?" He said, "I've been put on another project, they moved me down a few floors, to work in the lab, under the big Conference room. This part of the building is underground, it's restricted access, you won't even be able to enter without a badge."

"Ok, where does that put me then?" said Brick.

"I'm actually gunna have you shred old paperwork and clear out what is left in my old office." Said Pete. "You don't need special clearances to do so. That should take you a few hours. Afterward I want you to start looking for a Job, there is a phone book in my old desk. You can make calls from that office, or you can use the phone in the lobby and hang out with Sarah, the new receptionist."

They pull up to the main gate of *R&D Laboratories*, a mostly steel and glass structure, 4 stories in most parts, the building is almost fenced in by thick pine trees surrounding the property perimeter. Pete checks his watch as he pulls up to the guard shack.

The guard greets them, "Morning, Pete!"

"Good morning," said Pete. "Hey, have you seen Ben yet?"

"Dr. Bromine? Asked the guard, "No sir, I haven't seen him this morning."

"Ok, thanks anyway, have good one," says Pete before leaning over his steering wheel to scan the parking lot.

"You too, sir." Said the guard as he begins raising the fence arm.

They dry their feet and make their way through the lobby greeted by the smell of fresh donuts and the echo of Pete's shoe heels as they make their way to Sarah's desk.

Sarah says, "Good morning, Dr. Benson," bursting with a warm smile. "This must be one of our future engineers you've been telling me about?"

"Good morning, Sarah. Please, call me Pete, and Uh-uhh, Noo. This is my other son, Brick. He is going to be helping me out with some things today, before I leave him with you. He gets to look for his first job." Said Pete.

"Oh, Okay." Said Sarah. "Well, he's got your looks, very handsome. I'm happy to help, would either of you like a donut?"

Pete passes on the gesture, "Umm No, I still have all of those cookies, thank you. Brick?"

Brick doesn't hesitate and reaches for a donut with a bashful smile. "Thanks," he said.

"Anything else, Dr. Benson?" Sarah asks.

Pete sets his briefcase on the counter to pull out a folder of paperwork that he took home to finish the night before, something he's tired of doing. "Uh-yea, can you fax these to Diane, please? Oh, and when Ben comes in, can you have him drop my paper shredder off at my old office, please?"

"Sure thing," said Sarah, "And-uhh-Yeah, I'm pretty sure Dr. Bromine is already in. I don't think he left last night."

Pete, already walking toward the elevator door as Sarah says that, pauses to think for a moment and says, "hm...ok, thanks,"

The elevator door springs open, they step out to the left and into the hallway to see Pete's paper shredder, right outside his office door. "Would ya look at that," Pete says. "Man, it's too bad they have us on different projects now. It was really something working with Ben, what a character, I wonder what they have him working on...Okay, Brick, you know the routine. The dumpster is out back, the bags are in the drawer, and the phone book is in the desk. Here is my new extension, it's protocol not to pick up while doing load tests, so give it a few minutes before trying again."

"Woah," said Brick, as he glances around the office to see scattered plates of brownies, cookies, and pastries.

"Knock yourself out," said Pete. "I helped Sarah out with some of her college work, and now plates just show up. She hasn't said anything, But-uhh, I just don't know who else it would be. The cafeteria should be open in an hour if you want real food, you good?"

Brick, is still taking in all the treats says, "Uh-yeah, yea I think so."

Pete takes one more look around before leaving and says, "Ok, cool. See ya."

"See ya." Brick said before turning back around toward the desk, now overwhelmed with memories.

Among the scattered treats, sat a phone, a short stack of science magazines that sit under a lamp on one side of the desk. Along with a keyboard, mouse, and a CRT monitor on the other end of the desk. Three tall filling cabinets partially filled with documents on the wall to the left, followed by a tall lamp in corner that lit most of the room, then a waist high bookshelf spanned most of the back wall, now empty. Above that, from what Brick could recall here, used to be a frame of his dad's doctorate, accompanied by a few framed newspaper cutouts of his and the company's success over the years. The corner opposite the tall lamp had end table with a lamp on it that lit the rest of the room, and a chair each side of it.

He grabs enough paper to build a few hefty stacks that he sits on the desk, sits down on the squeaky old office chair and begins shredding paper. About 15 minutes goes by, you can smell the hot shredder from the hallways. As Brick tares off the bottle of oil taped to the side of the shredder to start oiling it, he hears the elevator ding. The ding was followed by the sound of somebody fumbling with some keys to open a door down the hall. Brick waits for a moment then disregards the noise and continues to shred and bag the paper.

Another 15 minutes or so goes by and more noise from down the hallway is heard. No elevator ding, just some thuds and bumping around followed by somebody talking. The talking leads to what sound a lot like somebody arguing over the phone, just one voice can be heard. This goes on for a minute and suddenly stops. Brick, having cleared out most of the cabinets has built a small blockade of bags built up by the door side. He decides to start running bags out to the trash, on his second round he notices a light glow from the bottom of a door down the hallway, right about where the noise was coming from.

He stands at the elevator door waiting for it to open as the light from the door down the hallway flickers and then goes back to steady glow. The elevator dings, he snaps out of daze and walks into the elevator with bags in hand. He makes his way back to the office after his trash run, shreds the last of the paper and make a couple more trips out to the dumpster, no noises or strange lights from anything down the hallway.

After the last run for trash, he stood outside the elevator door for a minute. He slowly looked back and forth at the dark, cloud filled window, at the end of the hallway to his left that his dad's old office is on and to the right where the mysterious glow and noise came from. The phone rings in his dad's old office. Startled, he hurries over assuming it's his father. "Hello?" he said. Sure enough, It's his father. Pete seems disappointed in the responses but quickly changes tone with his plans for the rest of the day.

"Brick?"

"Yea, what's up?"

"You find a job yet?"

"no."

"You eat all the cookies?"

"...no."

"You hangin' out with Sarah?"

"No, I'm in your old office."

"Oh...well, what have you been doing?"

"Uh...I shredded and got rid of all that old paper like you asked. I was just about to start looking for a job."

"...alright. Well, it's Friday. I have about another hour or so of testing, what do you say we take off early and pick up your brother and sister, so they don't have to walk home in the rain? That gives you some time to uh-find-uh, find a job, I guess."

"Ok, see you in the lobby?"

"Yup, see ya."

Brick heads down to the lobby, phone book in hand.

"Hey, you." Sarah said with a smile, "you find a job?"

"...no."

Sarah gladly hands him a pen, some paper, and recommends he start with some of the restaurants on his side of town. He spent the next hour or so before his dad made his way to the lobby, doing just that. Most didn't show any interest but quite a few of them at least took his info down and said that they'd reach out if something comes up.

Ch.2 Ha-ha...chickens

The next morning, Brick wakes up to his mother knocking on his bedroom door. "Brick, telephone...it's for you." Brick springs up and grabs the wireless house phone from his mother's hand, poking through the bedroom door. His mom makes her way back downstairs to get back to some laundry. His dad is on the couch bouncing between the TV and the paper, in between commercials. A few minutes later, Brick heads downstairs to put the phone back and his dad asks, "you get a call to go hang out?"

"No, I kind of got a job." replied Brick.

Pete is both excited and confused with Brick's response, "Kind of? got a job? you either did or didn't. Where at, who with, doing what?" he said.

"The *Iconic Taco*, John is the owner, he asked if I could move the dumpsters in and out Mondays and Thursdays. Pick up hours are 8-12, no one is there until just before 10 when they open, he doesn't want any of his employees wrestling with any dumpsters and then handling food. So, he's been heading in early to take care of it. I can pull them in and out on my way to and from school. I don't have a car, so that's all the work he could offer for now."

"Ok...so you-uh, found some work, that might lead to a job." Pete said as he stands up, walks into the kitchen, and returns to hand Brick a set of keys.

"These the keys to the truck?"

"Yup." Pete said before turning back around and heading toward the couch.

"I-uh...thought it wasn't running."

"It isn't." Pete says as he takes a set.

"...Thanks?" Brick said before heading into the kitchen.

"You're welcome."

Minutes later, you can hear the cereal puffs ping this side of Bricks dish as the sound of, "*BREAKING NEWS*" jumps from the television. "*'The Knock Outs'*, do it again!," Pete comments, "It's about time somebody starts coming down on these guys," about the same time Zack and Samantha shuffles downstairs. Moments later, Jackie heads back in from a little yard work. "Good morning," she said to the kids as she went for the sink.

Pete mutes the television before looking over and saying, "that everybody?" The kids, "Mhmm," as Jackie says, "yea."

"You got this, Jackie?" said Pete.

"...uh-h, yea...yea, I got this." She said. "I'm sure you've been wondering about your grandmother, Eloise. Your father said he broke the news to you already but I-I, I wanted to let you to know that a friend of hers will be by later with most of her belongings, it's really not much from what I gathered. The same friend that delivered the news, she used to stay with. She is supposed to be by later today, I-I don't know if I'm ready to deal with her belongings right now, I'd appreciate it if you kids helped me with it."

The kids looked around at each other just before Samantha comfortably spoke for everybody, "Of course, Mom."

"Thanks...I want you kids to help yourself to anything that interests you, I'm sure she would have wanted it that way. We can find a nice home for whatever is left."

The phone rings, Jackie answers. "It's for you Samantha, it's Kate." Samantha takes the phone and sneaks off upstairs. Jackie heads back outside for some fresh air and to tend to the garden. Pete unmutes the television, as Brick pokes around at what's left of his cereal, and Zack drops something to eat in the toaster. Brick brings up the truck.

"Zack, you wanna help me get the truck running?"

"No, not really. Why? What happened?

"I found, some—wait, no?"

"No, Brick. I don't *want* to...but I guess I could. Lemme eat something first."

Shortly after, they both made it outside to take a look at the truck. A few trips to the garage later, Zack lets the hood drop and close shut.

"...well, Zack?".

"Your screwed."

"Really? gee-thanks."

"So far, fuel pump, most likely a battery, and possibly an alternator. Fuel pump for sure."

Samantha now walks outside to let the two of them know that Kate is gunna be by around sundown to pick all of them up for the bonfire, before asking about the truck.

"I already got the okay to go, for all of us." she said. "Why are you guys messing with the truck?"

Brick replies, "We're trying to figure out what's up with it, dad gave me the keys."

Samantha says, "ha-ha, dad gave you a broken truck. You got money to fix it?"

"no."

"HA HA"

Jackie calls out just after Samantha laughs, "KIDS, Barbara is here."

They make their way to the front of the house to be introduced and bring their grandmothers belongings into the house. They spend some time talking to Barbara before she leaves, and they get to go through things. Pete sets her guns over to the side of the living room and Jackie steps out. Brick finds himself with a few boxes to go through, mostly camping gear. Samantha picks up one with more personal stuff, some journals, artsy nick-nacks, along with a smaller box of jewelry. She slips one on one of the bracelets, pokes around a little more before passing the box to Zack, who grabs a compass necklace before passing to Brick, who picks out a necklace with a fancy trinket, about the only masculine item left to be had. The only things left were a fishing pole, bow, some maps, and a few bags of clothes.

Brick throws an idea out, "What do you guys think about hiking one of these days like we used to with gram?" We could even camp out."

Samantha agrees and suggests next weekend. "Theres a few trail heads just up the way, where she used to stay."

Zack says, "Ok, yea, everything should be dried up by then."

Shortly after dinner, the doorbell Rings. It's Kate and Raj, there to pick them up. Everyone runs upstairs quickly to grab their jackets and bags before getting into the car. It wasn't long before they were at the beach smashing up a couple of old pallets to burn.

Raj and Kate give their condolences after hearing the news about the grandmother.

"Thanks," said Brick, "We're planning on going out on a hike next week, we might even camp. You guys should come."

They settle on a time to get together for their trip before Raj changes the subject, "Brick, thanks for having my back the other day...you don't wanna know what they're calling you now. Hey, what's up with the Asylum? Kate told me about it on the way over, I heard its haunted. My sister used to go there with her friends, back when she was still in high school. You guys really wanna go?"

Brick is quick to reply, "It's not haunted."

Samantha is even quicker to comment, "You don't know...He doesn't know." As she looks to Kate and joggles her head in doubt.

Kate says, "Well, I heard there's all sorts of stuff in it, even underground tunnels.", and Raj shares what he's heard.

"Yea, man. I heard a kid got so scared, he took off running down one of them, and ended up crawling out of a hatch down by another water tower a couple blocks away." he said.

That statement reminds Samantha share an opinion of hers, "Oh yea, Can you not park so far away when we go? you always park in Africa, somewhere."

Raj sees the importance and is quick to slam her opinion, "Uhh, it's in case we get rolled, man. We scatter and meet back up at the remote location with the vehicle, duh."

Kate agrees, "It does make sense."

And so does Zack, "Yea...it does." He says, before Raj continues on to share what he's heard.

"But I also heard that cops don't even want anything to do with the place, they won't get near it. There where all kinds of crazy experiments that went on back in the day, it's a different kind a haunted...next level spooky." He said.

Zack is tired of talking about it and decides to throw a match on the conversation and says, "You guys wanna go?" ...or just keep talking about it?"

Less than an hour later, they make their way over to the Asylum. First, they cruise by slowly and gaze through the chain link fence, past the scattered eerie trees and creepy looking pine, the kind that slump over just a bit at the peak. They find a place to park, a couple blocks away of course, before making their way back over on foot.

The bunch lines up at the fence and they all rest their hands up on the fence. With their fingers looped through the was cold, damp, and rusty chain links, and Samantha says, "...well?"

"Well, what? Said Brick, "You and Kate and are going first, it was your guy's idea. Unless your uhh...scared?"

The two girls looked at each before looking back through the fence at the old, distressed building that seemed to stare back at them. "Alright," both of them said as they shrugged their shoulders before glancing at each other once more and heading up over the fence. The boys followed them up and over the fence. They head behind the first set of buildings to get out a sight, so they can get their flashlights out and make their way into one of the buildings that is believed to have some of the more interesting medical equipment left.

The building they enter opens two stories inside and has a large run-down seating area that has clearly been overrun by squatters. The stars and clouds can be seen through a large square opening where a large glass window used to be directly centered on the roof top. At the end is a long hallway with a series of doors. A few toward the back seem to be untampered with as if people quit searching. The group stumbles across a strange room with a large table and what looks like recording equipment. One chair with restraints sat backed to the wall behind the big table with several standard chairs around the table, opposite of the door, and was bolted to the ground.

They walk through one afflicted room after another, mostly offices. With no luck finding any such equipment, before they decided to head back outside and explore deeper into the property.

Raj is having trouble recalling where he had heard some things were located and says, "I thought that was it...Let's try over here, I heard something about an old house."

"Let's try that one," Samantha says as she points to a building off in the distance.

Zack agrees and says, "Yea, that looks like it could pass for a house."

Sure enough, it was the house they had heard about. One of the windows was un-boarded and the boards over the front door were kicked out from the inside, making for an easy access. They made it through most of what feels like a war-torn, two-story house, straight out of a horror movie before heading back downstairs. Raj opens a door under the staircase that has another hatch door on the floor, already left open. "Yo", he says, "Check this out." Everybody gathered around, "a cellar?" Kate says, "or basement?" No one really seemed to have an answer, everyone was overwhelmed that the house they had heard about, was real, a lot more real than they imagined.

"...well?", said Samantha.

The boys shine their lights at her and Kate before both saying, "*WELL*?...after you."

The temperature seemed to drop significantly, as they dropped down the scuttle below the staircase. The compartment appeared to be used to an office at one time, it's not nearly as trafficked or distressed as the rest of the house or any other part of the property they have explored so far. It almost appeared occupied, everything extremely dated, but functional. Upon further exploring, they found what is most likely the hatch to the backyard, big enough to fit the furniture that was down there.

Theres also a very small restroom and another door. The door next to a bookshelf is stocked with an assortment of old audio recordings and looked like it was easily slid to cover it at some point. They filled a backpack up with some of the old cassettes, tapes, and reel-to-reels.

Zack says,"...Ladies first," with his hand out, after sliding the bookshelf over and revealing a passage door.

Kate responds, "C'mon, dude...really?"

Raj and Zack both start making chicken noises, waving their curled arms, and bobbing their heads while they cluck.

Samantha says, "Let's go, Kate." as she grabs her by the arm and heads toward the newly discovered passage. Brick flushes the toilet after sneaking over to the restroom just as they enter. Raj and Zack both screamed before dropping their flashlights.

"Ha-ha...chickens," said Samantha, before leading the group into the dark passageway.

The passage stretches about 10 feet before making a hard right and about another 25 with another door at the end, along with a passage to both left and right just before the door. They start to hear noise as they turn the first corner and wait. They notice light flicker and glow subtly around the door at the end of the passage. More noise comes from down the hall, a man's voice, they point their lights to the ground, it almost sounds like somebody is arguing. The light behind the door flickers and glows very bright again before completely blacking out, followed by some loud smashing noises. They panicked and turn around the way they came.

Samantha says, "Go-gog-gogogoo-goo," as softly as she can, now behind the entire group, trying best she can not to push them over each other.

They make the hard turn headed back toward the basement doorway and hear cracks and squeaks of floorboards from above the basement that room echo down into the passage they are in. They stop and wait for a second before Samantha whispers, "What do we do?"

Brick whispers back, "Go back that way, make a right, I think that way is toward the car at least, Go-googogoo-goo."

They run down the passage, hang a quick right before the door. With their lights, they see steps up ahead at the end of that passage, leading up. Moments later they come bursting out from a door at the end of that staircase, now in another building, down a way from where they started below. They see flashlights through a boarded-up window of the old house they started in. A helicopter off in the distance shines a light over the house before focusing on another building down the way.

"Raj, I thought you said the cops wouldn't get near this place?" said Brick.

"That's just what I heard, man.", Raj replies.

Zack scans the building before asking, "Where do we go from here?"

Brick points out one of the windows with the boards and glass busted out and says, "You see the water tower? We gotta get back on the other side of that, and get over the fence...C'mon, we're going through the window."

They take off running for the fence on the other side of the water tower. They managed to make it back to the car and get everyone back home.

Ch.3 Near and Dear

"Good morning," said Jackie, as she comes in the side door to the kitchen, "did you guys have a good time at the Bon fire?"

Brick replies, "Uhh-yea, yea it was cool."

Zack adds, "...yea, we had fun."

"Well, good." Jackie says," ...Sam made it home with you guys or is she staying at Kate's?"

Brick replies, "she's here, she's still in bed."

Jackie sets some things on the counter before saying, "Oh, okay. Well, breakfast is in the microwave and leftovers are in the fridge, if that doesn't do it." Before she heads back outside.

"Brick, you got the tapes from last night?", said Zack.

"No, I think Sam does, I don't have anything that will play them, do you?", replied Brick.

"Yea, I think I got something, I'm gunna go see if Sam is up." said Zack.

Over the next few hours, Zack figures out a way to start transferring the audio over to CD's. They begin listening and sharing the CDs throughout the next week, as Zack gets them transferred.

Thursday morning, the family is gathered in the kitchen as they usually do and Pete decides to ask about a few things, "You guys doing ok in school? No problems since your back, Brick?"

"Yea, everything has been good." Brick replied.

Pete is glad to hear that news, "Good...hey, how's work? you get to meet your boss yet?"

"Not bad, I just gotta make sure I leave a few minutes earlier and no, not yet. I'm supposed to meet up with him this afternoon." Brick replied.

"Ok...well uh, you be sure to let him know you got a set of wheels now, and that you're fixing it up, okay? Hopefully he doesn't decide to look for somebody else...I'm sure you and your brother will have in running in no time." said Pete.

"Will do." replied Brick.

Pete is reminded to bring something else up after flipping through the paper,"...Oh, Hey. You guys were out Saturday night, right? Did you guys notice anything strange going on? I've been reading about a string of grave robberies since then. A couple on Saturday night and a couple last night."

Brick pauses to think for a moment before responding, "No, nothing like that."

Pete folds his paper up before getting up from the table and says, "Alright, well you kids be careful out there, please. I gotta get going."

Later that day, Brick meets up with his new boss, John. Excited about the news of Brick's project, John decides to give him a few extra bucks to help get the old truck running.

"Look, kid. That's good news. I can't wait.", John said. "Your gunna come in real handy. I want you take this cash and get moving on your truck, would you do that for me?...here's the 20 for luggin' those dumpsters down the alley Monday and Thursday, keep the change. I'll see ya next week. Thanks, kid." before handing him a hundred-dollar bill.

Brick picks up a fuel pump that same day, it's installed by the next night. Samantha walks out to check on the boys working on the truck to make plans with them for the rest of the weekend.

"Do you guys still wanna go hiking this weekend? She asked, "Kate and Raj wanna know."

Brick replies, "Mmm...Yea, Zack and I are going to do a tune up tomorrow and check out a couple more things, how about Sunday?"

"Okay, sounds good. Oh, and those tapes got Kate thinking about some things, she wants to hit the library. I guess we can do that tomorrow while you guys work on the truck." said Samantha.

Sunday morning rolls around and the gang meet up for breakfast. Jackie makes flapjacks before sending them off with mystery bags of snacks and lunches.

The group makes their way to an old trail the grandmother used to take them too. They decide to look for an old waterfall they visited years back. Along the way, Brick asks to see maps that belonged to their grandmother.

Samantha thinks she recognizes the trail they are supposed to take and says, "I think it's that way." As she points of to the right of a fork in the trail they are approaching.

Brick disagrees before suggesting that they take a look at the maps, "I don't think so, look at that tree, I think I'd remember that tree, do you?" He said as he points at a very large tree with a gaping hole in the side.

Samantha pulls out the maps and starts to go through them, "I don't know where these are for, there aren't any names, besides most of them all look hand drawn. There are some symbols though." She said.

Brick is in disbelief and wants to see the maps himself, "What? Lemme see, there's gotta be something." He said before the group huddles around the maps.

Zack notices something as Brick is scanning one of the maps and says, "What's that?" As he points to a spot on the bottom of the map.

Brick replies, "I don't know, it kinda looks like a house."

Zack tilts his head to the side before grabbing the map himself and explaining it. "Yea, turn it to the left, if that's north, and her place was down here where that house is...then this should be the fork we're at. We have to make a left and head up toward whatever that symbol is."

They get to the waterfall and decide to take a break for lunch. Samantha and Kate discover a recess behind the waterfall, they find that it leads further back, before opening up.

"Sam, did you bring a light?" asked Kate.

Samantha replies, "No, let me go see if the boys did." Before heading back out and calls out to the boys, who are sitting on a large rock across from the plunge pool. "Hey, did one of you guys bring a light?"

Raj is sure that his bag has a couple lights but is confused because it's still daylight out and says, "Yeah, why? what's up?"

"Come here, we found a cave behind the waterfall." Samantha replied.

They end up in the cave. Raj pulls out a camping lamp that he sets in the middle of the cave. Zack spots something etched into the wall, by the entrance of the cave. "Brick, turn around...look." He said as he points to the symbol.

Brick pulls out the map they had out earlier that had a house and another symbol that they didn't recognize. He unfolds it and says, "It's the same."

Samantha recalls something and says, "Wait a second...Brick, come here. let me see that necklace."

Brick takes off the necklace and hands it to Samantha.

"It's the same symbol," she said as she held it up to the etching in the cave.

Kate asks, "What do you think it means?"

Samantha says, "I don't know but it's got something on the back." before reading the back of the trinket aloud.

"Keep it Near and Dear, Be Sure the Coast is Clear."

She repeats it aloud, a slow a few times.

Brick has an epiphany after repeated it a few times himself and says, "...near and dear...SAM, hold it to the wall."

Samantha holds the necklace to the wall as everyone watches. Nothing seemed to happen. Samantha turns around toward the rest of the gang to see that the cave wall opposite of them has changed. "Guys...look." as she points.

They turn to look and respond with the same, "Woah."

Everyone slowly walks over toward a new recess on the other side of the cave, where it appears as if some of the rock had just vanished. The Recess is an opening of another passage that leads to another cavern like the one they are in now. On the other side is a similar entrance with a subtle glow of daylight and the sound of water pouring down, echoing through the chamber.

They continue past the waterfall and find themselves in an entirely different world. It lies between the foothills of two mountains, to the left and right. The lake appears to have other streams that lead in from surrounding mountains and narrows backdown, way off in the distance. To the right, tucked up and burrowed into the foothill, is a cabin. It looks almost as if the mountain had slowly been melting over it.

The mountains are covered richly with pine and boulders. The group lines up at the gorge in awe and stare off in the distance. They stare out from the rocks for a moment before hopping down the rocks, into the lush, green meadow, surrounding a lake about quarter mile downstream.

Brick focuses in on the cabin for a moment before asking Samantha for the maps. After skimming through a few of them he finds another map that has a house symbol like one of the other maps and points it out to the gang. "This is the only other map with one of those little house symbols...if that's the house...and that's the lake...then this should be us right here. Don't you think this is kind of odd?" he said.

Raj replies, "Uh...which part, man? the part about the houses?...or uhh...the part that we just found another world inside of a cave?"

Zack agrees with Raj and says, "Yeah...which part, Brick?"

"Well...both, I guess. Hey, where did Sam and Kate go? said Brick.

Raj notices the girls climbing down some rocks to their side, "Looks like they are already heading down that way." He said.

The boys hurry down the rocks to catch up with the girls.

Brick calls out to them, "Hey, wait up. You sure you guys wanna go down there?" Before him and the rest decide to follow along. They head down to a trail that runs along the stream, then runs around the lake before it cuts back up toward the foothill and over toward the house.

Zack says, "Look at the chimney... looks like somebody is home. You gunna walk up and knock on the door?"

Brick replies, "Well, we aren't gunna throw rocks at the window, besides I don't see a doorbell...do you?"

The group makes it up to the porch and Samantha walks up to give the door a few good knocks. With no immediate response, Raj says very quickly, "Okay, let's go," just before the door cracks open. "Who is it?," sounds a man's voice through the crack of the door.

Samantha replies after no one else seemed to know what to say, "Uhh, friends of Eloise...well, her grandkids, and some friends. Did you know her?" she said.

The door swings open quickly, "You know where El is?", asked the man.

"Uh, noo...I'm sorry but she's no longer with us. It sounds like you two knew each other though, we are her grandkids, and these are friends of ours." said Samantha.

"...Please, come in. My name is Simon, and yes, El and I have been friends for many years...I figured something had happened to her, she left a few weeks back, she said she'd be back in a few days...she had always said not to come looking for her.", Said Simon.

Simon brings them into the house and into the den to sit and talk, Brick asks, "She Stayed here, with you?...I mean how did you meet?"

"Yes...we were on a raid, years ago. I was ambushed and badly injured. She saved my life...your grandmother was a great healer." said Simon.

Brick pauses to think before asking, "...healer?"

"Yes, a shaman. One of the best, every bit as good as any priest or cleric out there." said Simon.

Again, Brick pauses to think before responding, "Wait, what?"

Simon senses something about the confused faces he is looking at and says, "I take it she never brought you kids here, or shared anything with you, did she?

"No," Brick replies, "We lost touch with her in recent years, how do you end up here?"

"I inherited this place, my family was from your realm too, my parents were killed in a savage witch hunt when I was 8. I left that world and told myself I'd never return." Said Simon.

Samantha asks, "Your parents where witches?"

"No, they were Druids, shape shifters...your world calls a lot of magical things they don't understand or agree with, a Witch. Did you guys' care to stay for dinner?" said Simon.

Brick replies, "No, actually I think we were actually going to head out soon, it's still gunna be pretty late by the time we make it back home."

"Oh, ok...well, you'll have to come back soon, I'll have to show you around a bit...by the way, how did you find me?" said Simon.

Brick gestures to Samantha for the maps, already anticipating Simon would like to seem as he says, "We noticed a house marked on our grandmother's maps."

"Maps?...mind if I take a look at them?" asked Simon.

Samantha hands over the bundle of maps to Simon, he clears a table and begins looking at them.

"These look like some of her favorite places, what do you say we check some of these places out?" he said as he pulls a single map out, sliding it from the middle outward with his hands on the table, then setting some items down on the corners to keep it from rolling up.

"How about we start here, with *Paladin's Peak*? She loved this place...it will take us most the day to get there on horseback, but we shouldn't have any problem making it there on time, assuming we don't have any issues. We can celebrate her life there. What do you say?", said Simon.

The gang looks around at each other before Samantha replies, "I don't know how to ride a horse."

After everyone stares at Samantha for a moment before Zack says, "None of us do, Sam."

Samantha says, "Well, we still don't have any horses and I didn't see any on our way in."

Simon begins rolling the maps back up and says, "That's because they like to stay near a cave on the other side of the lake." He explains a few things he felt was important before getting back to the horses, "There are emergency escape passages through the den and down the other living quarters to my left if anything were to ever happen. They will lead you out to a few sets of release hatches scattered along the foothill. The one to our left exits out over where you guys came from. It will give you a good get-away start back home or you can cross the stream and circle the lake where the horses are. We only have 4 horses, 2 of you can ride doubles and one ride alone, you guys can take turns...well?"

The gang looks to each other once more before Brick replies, "Uhm, yea. I'm sure we can be back next weekend."

Ch.4 Paladin's Peak

"Bring it back, bring it back, a little further," said John, "That's it, right there, Brick." as he backs him into the rear loading area behind the restaurant. "That's some truck, kid. I used to have one back in the day, a lot like this, wasn't a crew cab though...Ok, I ordered new tables and chairs. I don't know if I told ya, but I got two other spots. I own the deli down on 5th and another off Pine, in old town. Split 'em up between the two stores, leave the old ones out in back for now, please. I'll uh, see ya Thursday, I may have you help me with a Fryer. Be careful out there, alright?...Thanks, kid."

Friday morning, Pete gets at call in the middle of breakfast. "I gotta go, the power went out again in the lab, its running off the back up...it's the second time this week. I don't know what's going on. It's not our department, nobody is supposed to be in this early. Your mother said you guys are staying over at Raj's and will be taking off early in the morning to go camping. Have fun, be careful...Oh, Brick...Ben wanted to know if your arm was broken? he was waving at you somewhere off of 5th street the other day, you didn't wave back."

Brick replied, "What?"

"I guess you had a bunch of chairs n' what not in the back?...anyhow, he drives that old burgundy bucket, still. Pay attention out there, please." said Pete.

The kids decide to make their way back to Simon's right after school instead of leaving Raj's first thing in the morning.

Simon is there to greet them. "Well, I wasn't expecting you guys tonight, it's probably better ya did though, it'll give us a nice early start. I hope you like fish and sugar snaps. I didn't plan on having anyone over for dinner." He said.

Simon shows them where to get cleaned up and ready for bed. He is a little excited and has a hard time sleeping. So, he spends the evening fishing, gathering, and getting the rest of the bags packed for their trip.

Simon managed to find some fresh eggs and fruit to go with to go with some oats. The gang heads out first thing, after breakfast.

The kids take off through the meadow, and circle around the lake, to the first cavern they find tucked away in a cove. There they see two horses standing at the entrance. The kids spend a little time investigating the cave entrance and find Simon's safe house, along with a third horse. A few minutes later, Simons rounds the corner of the cove, "I see you guys met, Daisy and Disco." he said.

Samantha replies, "Yea and another in the cave."

Simon asks, "White mark that runs down his whole face?"

"No." said Brick.

Simon says, "Oh, then I guess you've also met Millie. I'm not sure where Bolt is." Before letting out a loud whistle. "give it a minute."

The sound of sticks and branches are heard breaking off in the distance before trotting hooves begin to near the cove. Moments later, Bolt rounds the corner. "Ahh-there he is, he's blind by the way. Your grandmother rode this horse, they got along very well. He's got an extraordinary sense of hearing and smell...I'll be riding him for now." Said Simon.

Zack had been looking around the cove before Simon arrived and asked, "Hey, what are these big lines that run down from the mountain side?"

"Uhh-those are power lines," said Simon. "They run to a mill generator just before one of the grand falls. The power switch is on the other side of that rock, just follow the wires back, you'll find it."

Brick follows the wires back and pulls up on the large hand switch, turning the power on. The dim yellowish lights slowly fade on, pulsing a couple times before becoming steady. The cave has a large raised wooden deck you can easily walk under that runs along the cave wall and another loft area above that. There are several workstations, scattered tools and equipment, along with a large piece of equipment that is sitting in the center with a tarp over it.

They walk around and breathe in the moist air that reeks of old damp lumber and gear oil, used for the mill generator before Simon shows them where to find some things for their trip.

"Okay, the saddles n' what not are on the wall above the store barrels. Let's get you kids riding, we have a long day ahead of us." said Simon.

Zack peaks under the tarp at the equipment and asks, "Hey, Simon. What's this?"

"Nothing." Simon replies, "It doesn't work, alright?"

Zack can tell that Simon really isn't interested in talking about whatever is under the tarp but persists anyhow, "Well, what is it though?" he asked.

"It's an Anti-Gravity Aircraft, Okay?...I won it in a card game, it cost me more to get it here than its probably worth though." said Simon.

Zack gets a better understanding of why it's such a touchy subject after he asks, "What's wrong with it?

"I don't know, neither does the Orc I won it from. Some gnomes were supposed to come look at it last week. They never showed. I have to talk to them next time I go to Bruiser's." said Simon.

Zack asks about Bruiser's instead of leaning on Simon for more details or offering to help with it.

"*Bruiser's Bazaar,*" Simon says, "It's the biggest marketplace around, I'll have to take you guys the next time I go, you'll get a kick out of it...Lets go, we're wasting daylight."

They spend a short while getting used to riding horses. They make their way back out around the lake, back toward the cabin. Simon begins explaining the area.

"You see the opening in mountains to left on the other side of the lake? That's our valleys grand fall. All the surrounding streams will lead to this lake here and drop from there. The streams all lead up to other realm portals. We will be going up to the fourth stream from the cabin for *Paladin's Peak*, we go up the second to get to Bruiser's." he said.

The group makes it up into the cavern that leads to *Paladin's Peak*, they enter the realm and step into a very dry hot canyon side. The canyon walls are varying shades of reds, purples, and yellows with a river at the bottom, several hundred feet below. The climb up the canyon side only takes a minute or two that leads them to flat open ground with hills, way off in the distance.

"Welcome to the *Badlands of Devore*," said Simon. "This side of the canyon is *Eastern Badlands*; the other is *Western Badlands*. Those hills off in the distance are where we have to go."

They spend a couple hours following the canyon cliffside several miles down to the hills where they begin climbing.

Simon looks up at the mountain side and says, "Perfect."

Brick asks, "What's perfect?"

"Perfect timing, I think we're gunna make it, right on time." Simon responds with subtle excitement.

They spend a couple more hours climbing up the rocky mountain side, up to the top just as the sun begins to set. The group sets their bags down and walks over toward the cliff side of the canyon. Off in the distance, across the canyon is a giant tree that competes with the mountains that fall behind it, lining the horizon. The top of the sky begins to darken and show stars as the sun sets, while the sky above the mountains slowly fades into similar colors of the canyon walls below.

Simon takes a look around and says, "Let's set up camp, there should still be a few pieces of firewood on the other side of that rock over there, let me know if you guys want help setting up."

Brick says, "I think we should be good, what did you have in mind for dinner?...salmon?"

Simon replies, "Yes, and I also brought boars meat. I usually stash meat in the snowpack on the mountain above the cabin, I was up early enough to hike up there."

Raj is excited to be holding up something that resembles a cactus limb and says, "Sounds good. Hey, what's this?"

Simon replies, "Mmm—I don't know what it's called, but I wouldn't eat it, if that's what you're thinking?"

Immediately disappointed, Raj slowly lowers the limb in his hand and says, "...ok."

It takes a few moments for Simon to realize that everyone is hungry and has been for some time. He quickly figures that it would best to gather some nearby edible plants to add to their meal so that they don't blow through all their food.

"You that hungry?" asked Simon. "Okay. Well, those plants you just had should have pink and yellow flowers that bloom from them, with thick meaty bulbs. You should be able to eat the bulbs, I remember seeing quite a few on the way up here."

The kids gather a bunch of bulbs before sitting down at the fire and begin eating. By now, the sun has just about set, leaving a bold silhouette of the massive great oak tree. It's backed by a colorful glowing sky over the mountains.

Samantha says, "Wow, that's pretty,"

Kate agrees and says, "I see why your gram liked it here."

Simon is glad to see that everyone seems to be enjoying themselves and says, "Just wait, the best part is coming up."

A few minutes pass, the aurora begin to fade in and out over the horizon, the sky is full of stars. Faint green lights start to surface along the badlands across the canyon and begin to take off into the air before circling around the Great Oak.

A moment later, Zack asks,"...Fireflies?"

"Yea, big ones." Simon says, "Big enough to fly off with somebody, be careful."

Samantha's attention is still fixed on the massive, lone, Great Oak. "Why does that tree look dead?" she asked.

Simon replies, "Uhh—because it is. It's a petrified great oak. I don't know if you can see the tiny little trees surrounding it now that it's dark out, can you? Those are normal oak, that great big oak used to be home to a colony of wood elves, however many thousands of years ago. It's now a Necromancer den, they've been using it as a castle."

The Great Oak is now illuminated between the swarm of large fireflies, the aroura overhead, and the stars poking through the black skies that shimmer above.

Brick asks, "Are necromancers bad?"

Simon replies, "That calling is definitely on the darker side of the magic spectrum, if that's what you're asking? In this particular case, yes. With these rogue necromancers I know that if a bounty is high enough for them, then they'll turn on their own. There has been a few known to do some good though."

Simon goes on to share an experience during a raid before answering other questions.

Brick asks, "Do you have a calling, Simon?"

"No, not really. I wanted to train with the Monks, but they refused to train me. Rather than push my luck with them and risk being tormented or feared, I went to Bruiser's and enlisted with a Cyb-Orc faction, I became a marksman. " said Simon.

Zack is intrigued with both the Monks and the term feared, vagally recalling the words in some of the audio he had transferring from the Asylum. "What do you mean torment or feared?" he asked.

Simon replies, "The Monks have a reputation to mentally mutilate anyone who challenge them, good or bad. They don't recognize good or evil, they will only train you if they see you are fit for it. They are known as *The Monks of Mayhem* because of this; having trained and forged some of the greatest warriors on both sides of the spectrum. They do not desire riches or material items, only respect. There is no way of knowing whether they will choose to work with you in advance.'

'They hyper-train telepathically, often cramming thousands of hours of training, into just hours or minutes, with things like swords, axes, bows, and martial arts. However, they can use this same method to torment and torture you mentally, thousands of hours, in just minutes. The darker arts like necromancers have been known to cast fear spells that cause some pretty serious mental damage as well. But nothing compares to what to Monks are capable of." He said.

Samantha now begins to recall the term and says, "...fear spell?...fear spell. I remember hearing something about that in some of the recordings we found at the asylum."

A place immediately comes to mind for Simon, "That old psychiatric hospital?" he asked.

Samantha is surprised and replies, "Yea, how do you know about it?"

"My uncle spent the last few years of his of his life there. It was basically a prison for anyone caught or believed to be practicing magic, along with mentally ill. That's if they weren't killed or run out a town. It was also a place where they kept people that were victims of dark magic, like those that suffered from fear spells. Sometimes friends or family that have returned from other realms are damaged mentally, for one reason or another. Not everyone can function normally after they've been exposed to things that go on in other realms, lesser or greater realms." said Simon.

"Ok," said Samantha. "Well, That helps make some sense with what's on some of those tapes we found there."

Simon has an idea of what kinda things they could have heard, "Oh, I'm sure of it." He said, "To be honest, I had my concerns about showing you guys around. You really haven't reacted poorly to anything, so far." Then looked to Brick and asked," Did you guys bring those maps with you?"

"Yea, lemme grab them for you." replied Brick.

Simon starts to go through the maps and pauses and at couple before making it to one that he loses himself in.

Brick isn't sure what to make of his facial expression and asks, "Simon, you alright?" You have this look on your face, did we mess up that map?"

Simon quickly snaps out of it and replies, "No...no, not at all. Sorry, I must have overlooked this map before. It brings back some memories is all," Before rolling the maps up and setting them aside. "We are gunna need a little more than a weekend for that one." He said.

The kids look to each other for a moment before Samantha says, "Well, spring break was our last big break. We're probably gunna have to wait til' summer, assuming none of us end up with summer school...Brick." Due to Brick's grades landing him in summer school the last few years.

Simon thinks for a moment before saying, "Ok, then we can figure out another time for that adventure...I have somethings to catch up on before I'm ready to go to Bruiser's, I won't be able to take you along for the ride, what do you say we make plans for the weekend after next?"

The gang reminds Brick that with work he's the only one with any real obligations outside of school that could keep them from going. Since his routes fall in the week and his moves have so far, Brick replies, "Alright, sounds good, Simon."

Ok, cool. Simon says, "Let's hope nothing come up before then. I'm gunna turn in, I'll see you in the morning. And-uhh, be careful...I was serious about fireflies."

Ch.5 Why'd you drop it?

Thursday morning rolls around and the family is gathered in the kitchen. Pete asks Brick a few things before heading off to work.

"Brick, how's the truck running?"

"Uhh—pretty good, I'v been running errands all over town with it, seems fine."

"Good, you guys don't have any plans this weekend, do you?"

"No, we had something in mind for next weekend, what's up?"

"I want to pick up a couple 2x4's to take care of the back fence Saturday morning."

"Ok."

"Good. Well, I'm gunna head out, I see you kids later, be careful out there."

Pete heads over to the office and overhears Sarah on the phone while he waits in the lobby to discuss some details with her.

"...No, nothing has come in, I'll have to check back with them...No, they aren't open yet, I'm sorry...yes, I understand...I will...did you get any rest last night?...Hello?...Hello?" said Sarah.

Sarah hangs up the phone and says to Pete, "Good morning, Dr. Benson, I didn't notice you there."

"Good morning, Sarah. Can you get these to Diane? and these 2 pages only over to Carol, please?" said Pete.

"Sure thing. Oh, can you go check on Dr. Bromine? That was him on the phone. He's got a big presentation today and I think he could use your help with something. He's been waiting on Kal-Tek for some documents." Said Sarah.

"Yea, no problem, I'll go check on Ben, right now." Said Pete.

Pete makes his way over to Ben's office. As the elevator door opens, he notices some yelling down the hallway toward Ben's office. He waits and moment and then proceeds down the hall to knock on his door.

"Ben...BEN," Pete said before knocking again. "Ben, you alright?"

"Sarah?" Ben calls out before opening the door, "Oh, Pete, it's you. Sorry, I'm expecting some documents."

"I heard. Sarah asked me to check on you...was that you yelling?" said Pete.

Ben replies, "Uhh—yea, I-uhh...I was, I was on the phone."

Pete can tell that Ben is a little out of it and asks, "You okay?"

"Yea...yea, just-uh, got a lot going on."

"What did you want help with?" asked Pete.

"...nothing, Pete. I think I'm just gunna have to reschedule." replied Ben.

"Ok. Well, lemme know. I'll see ya later." Said Pete.

Pete continues with his workday and heads home. Saturday morning Jackie has a large breakfast ready before everyone is up. Pete makes his way downstairs first. "Woah...did I forget something?" he said.

Jackie replied, "What?"

"Is today something special?" Pete asked, "maybe I'm forgetting something. You got enough to feed a small army here."

"No, you guys are going to be working in the back today, right?" said Jackie.

Pete stares at the table of food replies, "Yea...it's just Brick and I. We gotta replace a couple 2x4's. It's gunna take us longer to go get them, then it is to put them in." said Pete.

"Well, you're not gunna starve doing it." Said Jackie.

"I guess not" Pete said as Brick comes down the stairs. "Oh, good. You're up. Help me put a dent in this before we get ready for the store, they should be open in about an hour."

They head down to pick up the wood from a store on 5th St., not far from one of the Deli's that Brick has been delivering to.

Brick asks, "Is that Dr. Bromine's Car?" As he points out toward a *Psychic's Fortune and Palm Reading* office.

"Oh yea, that's Ben's car alright...that's kinda strange for him to be there though." Said Pete.

Brick says, "Well, he's been there quite a bit, lately. I see him parked there when I'm delivering."

Pete is surprised to hear that and asks, "Really?"

"Yea, I saw him hugging some lady at the door the other day before he went over to his car. I honked but he didn't turn around." Said Brick.

"Huh...yea, he's had a lot going on lately, he didn't look very good the other day...Pull in the second driveway over there, it'll be easy to load if we park in the back." Said Pete.

Later the following week, the gang decides to head off to Simons after school on Friday. They manage to make it there with daylight left and discover that Simon is nowhere to be found in his cabin. They set their belongings down and decide to explore a little more in hopes that they will find him. The girls find a couple of large book shelfs filled with books in one of the living quarters, and the boys end up in the den staring up at some of the various weapons up on display.

Kate is skimming through a survival handbook she had pulled from one of the bookshelves. "Hey, Sam. Check this out." She Said.

Samantha walks over to look at the book Kate has in her hand and notices another set afterword, "what's this?" As she grabs a large, tattered book, one of a group similarly suited and begins skimming through it with Kate.

Kate says, "I don't know. They're cool looking books but I don't know what language any of it is, do you?

Samantha replies, "Mmm—nope." Before hearing a loud sound come from the front. Followed by a thud in the den from one of the boys dropping something.

The two girls look to each other for a moment before Samantha says,"...Hello?"

Simon comes walking through the front door and says, "Hey, guys. Your early. I was out on the other side of the lake. I wanted to make sure I would have dinner for you this time around, hope ya like duck." He walks down into the den to see Brick and Raj, both trying to place a rather heavy sword back up on the wall. Samantha and Kate both walking into the den, books in hand.

Simon looks around at everyone and says, "I uh—I see you guys made yourself at home. Find anything interesting?"

The group looks around at each other, a little disappointed in themselves.

Brick says, "Well, you do have a lot of neat stuff, Simon. Sorry, we were looking for you and got distracted."

Simon isn't bothered by their curiosity. He looks to the girls and says, "Those books you have in your hands aren't mine, they belonged to your grandmother." Before heading toward the boys to set somethings down. "That sword is coming with us to Bruiser's, you can go ahead lean it up against the wall. Here, catch." He says as he throws a few sets of ears tied together to Brick.

Brick catches and holds the pair up by string and asks, "What are these for?"

"A bounty...Should be a nice little chunk of change. It took me all last week to hunt the last guy down. El and I took this job up a while ago, her and I landed the first two guys together." Said Simon.

Samantha asks, "Gram was a Bounty Hunter?"

"Yea, a pretty good one too." Simon replied, "It's how we paid for most things. We both wanted to breed and sell mounts but never quite got around to it."

Brick asks, "Why are we taking that sword to Bruiser's, Simon?"

"We can buy, sell, and trade at Bruiser's, I wanna put this new one up one up the wall...If you guys like that, wait til' you see what's in the cellar." Said Simon.

Simon takes them down to his massive cellar that's burrowed into the mountain to take a look at the collection of arms, armor, and hunting gear. "We really should make use of the daylight, go ahead pick whatever you guys wanna use to chop up wood." he said.

The bunch grabs an assortment of swords and axes, except Brick. He seems to be mesmerized by a bow. Everyone begins leaving the cellar as he stands there admiring the craftsmanship of a bow he has in his hands.

Samantha looks back and asks, "How you gunna chop wood with that, Brick?

Simon looks back after hearing Samantha to see Brick with the bow and says, "Bring it...and a quiver, they're in the bin, over on the right."

They head outside to start chopping wood out front. They all take turns cutting wood with each weapon and begin bringing some of the pieces ready into the house.

Simon asks, "Where's that bow?"

Brick replies, "On the other side of that log, over there."

"Well, grab it." Said Simon," And unless you think you can hit the snow pack up on the mountain, you should just aim it at the lake."

Brick asks, "Why can't I just aim at a tree over there?"

"You could, it's probably better ya didn't though," said Simon.

Brick grabs an arrow and readies to shoot the arrow, as he draws back the tip of the arrow seems to suddenly ignite and catches on fire. He drops the bow and turns around with a startled look on his face.

Simon says, "Why'd you drop it?" before chuckling.

Brick replies, "You didn't see it catch on fire?"

"Mmm—yea, I didn't tell ya to aim it at the lake because I thought you'd be a bad shot. I just didn't want you to burn the whole forest down." Said Simon.

Simon lets the group take turns shooting the flaming arrows off into a hill only asking them to leave him one. He fires the last one off into the air, way atop the hill at a clump of snowpack. They decide to get a head start on tomorrow by bringing everything over to the cave and stable area, before sitting down for dinner.

"Zack, you mind passing the snaps, please?" asked Simon.

"Sure," Zack says, "Hey, Simon. What was that green cylinder up on the loft with shiny metal rings for?"

"It's part of a reactor...for a portal." Replied Simon.

"For other realms?" asked Zack.

"Yea...the portal you guys came through was made by the elders. Your key is an heirloom key. They were made to secure passage between lesser and greater realms. Methods to reproduce the portals have been achieved, some have reproduced with magic and others found a way to do it through technology. It's not easy either way.'

'Bruiser's is centered around the *Hall of Realms*, he seized control and fought to keep it a neutral ground around all factions and territories across realms to bring peace. All unsanctioned battles and duels must be done elsewhere, or you, your faction, even your realms can become blacklisted, in order to keep peace. Your name will immediately be put up with a bounty. It's not uncommon for factions or realms to deliver the heads of those who have been the cause for the blacklisting, as an apology in order to return." Said Simon.

Brick asks, "So, those ears...were they from someone caught fighting at Bruiser's?

"No, they were caught stealing from a vendor at Bruiser's...They were hiding in another realm...So, did you find any books that interest you?" said Simon.

Samantha replies, "Yes, but we can't understand a lot of them."

"Mmm—the fancy looking ones? Said Simon.

"...yea," replied Samantha.

"Well, I wish I could help you. I believe they're magic books. Again, most of those were your grandmothers...should be a pretty wide range too. I don't even know what dialects those are. We might be able to find someone at Bruiser's that can help though...I know there used to be some girls there that spoke of teachings, we'll have to ask around when we're there." Said Simon.

Ch.6 Bruiser's Bazaar

"Going once! going twice! Sold! to the gentleman in the back!" calls out an auctioneer, off in the distance as the group makes they're way out of the *Hall of Realms* within the busy courtyard interior of Bruiser's, teeming with a wide range of lifeforms.

Simon says, "We meet back here at the clock if we get split up. First, I wanna find those gnomes. If they aren't going to stop by I wanna get my deposit back. Oh, and keep your eye out for a big green frog running around in chain mail, his name is Jabadak. I want to get those gloves we packed last night back to him."

The inner wall of the Courtyard is lined with temporary vendors and merchants under tarps, across from them are fixed shops with more permanent locations. The group quickly scans the lower level where the gnomes would normally be, with no luck. Simon decides to collect on his bounty before running down his checklist. The group continues back around the large hallways that wrap around the courtyard and are bombarded with robust aromas varying from foods, botanicals, and smiths.

The kids notice a weapons range outside, they stand and watch a troll and ogre take turns throwing axes down range. Next to the range appeared to be a sparing area for close quarter weapons. Simon stops in to see an armor vendor to trade some of the old hides he had been saving up in exchange for repair work to some of his own gear.

Simon says, "Looks like we have a few hours to kill before I have to be back to pick up my bracers, are you guys hungry?"

Raj quickly replies, "We walked by something that smelled really good before we went over by the mounts."

"Probably the bison, let's go see." Said Simon.

They enjoy bison and potato skins as they hang back out next to some of the mounts penned up outside. Sets of dragons and very large great owls begin to circle overhead as groups on the ground start asking people to clear out around the pen areas.

Kate notices they are equipped with riding gear and asks, "Are they going to land those here?"

Simon replies, "Yea, it looks like they are out for practice races...they race around the peninsula, here."

"It's too bad we can't ride them."

Simon points to another area where mounts are sold and says, "No, but anything on this side you can ride...hippogriffs, great wolves, even the cockatrice."

Knowing that they have no intention of purchasing, Simon works out a deal with the trainers so that the kids can ride a few of the mounts.

"As long as they keep them grounded," Is what the trainers said.

...Their rides were short lived, as it was difficult to keep them grounded.

They made their way to the bank afterward, only to be sidetracked by the music that spilled from a bard's store. A short while is spent playing with various instruments before they continue to the bank. Simon asks one about the gnomes before leaving the bank where he is directed to the post.

Simon asks, "Have any of you seen the service gnomes that used to be by the post office?"

"No," replied one of the fairy clerks behind the counter ask they all look to each other.

One directly in front of him asks, "Have you checked the post office?

Simon replies, "No...I'll go ask, thanks."

The post office clerk says, "Nothing has been in or out for them in the last month and they haven't registered for a spot in the bazaar for about the same."

Something Simon overhears at the post office that reminds him to ask about the books. The man at the post office tells him to check upstairs.

"*The Beast & The Priest* is next to the locksmith and the *'The Seven Sisters'* is by the watch guy." He said.

The group heads upstairs in search of the stores. Simon reads off a sign as they round the first corner. "There it is, *'The Beast & the Priest'...Magic and Botanicals.*"

A thick odor of incense and botanicals spills from the door as they enter. A couple birds sound before taking off down the narrow shop toward the back. The back shelves are stocked with lamps and linens with beads and amulets strung along overhead.

The shopkeeper says, "Hello and welcome, what brings you in today?" as he stands up behind the long counter where it's lined with charm bags, candles, and carving tools. He makes his way toward the front of the store and stands behind a portion of the counter that is stocked with botanicals and condition oils.

Samantha asks, "We'd like to see if you could help us with some books, please?"

The man replied, "Of course, right this way." And began heading toward a section in the store where some books are kept.

Samantha says, "Oh, no. Uhh-we have some books we would like you to take a look at...please. We aren't sure what language they are."

Samantha pulls three books out from her bag and sets them on the counter.

The man takes a glance at the books and says, "Ah-yes, this here is Elven...I can't say for the other two."

"You speak Elvish?" asked Samantha.

The man replied, "No, but I do recognize the script...a couple of our botanicals are Elven. This is a Priest's shop. Mostly common tongue, here. Perhaps one of *the sisters* would be of more help. If I'm not mistaken, they have an elf or two in house and they're just around the corner. They also cover a much broader variety of magic."

They spend a few minutes looking through the store before heading to their next stop.

"Welcome to *'The Seven Sisters'*...what can we do for you?" a voice calls out from a woman at the back of store.

"Hello?" said Simon aloud as the group nears the back of the store, passing several racks of gowns and garments toward the voice.

"Yes?" says the woman as she springs out from a wall of garments she had been trying to get arranged.

Samantha says, "Hi, we were wondering if you could help us with some books that we have?"

"Certainly. Please, right this way," the woman says as she gestures and begins moving toward one side of the shop. "Let's see them," she said as she grabs her glasses off the countertop she is now standing behind. Samantha sets the 3 books upon the counter and lays the bag aside.

The woman says in a joking tone, "What makes you think I could be of help with this?" is it the ears?"

Samantha replied, "Uhh, no. We were told you may be able to help us."

Another woman's voice calls out from just outside the front store, "Mialee...Mialee, can you help us with these boxes?" Mialee hurries to help, almost knocking off a staff lined up along the wall with a series of others. "Be right there," as she rounds the display cabinet running along the back where it is stocked with assorted potions and elixirs.

The sound of goblets clank around in one box just as the mortar and pestles chatter with each step from another box. The woman proceeds to the other side of the counter to set the boxes down.

"Sorry about that...this is Shevette and Ayenna. Oh, and I am Mialee, sorry for not introducing myself." Said Mialee. "Where is Saylinn?

"Still out with Baba Olya," replied Shevette, the Feline Humanoid said as she begins pulling from the boxes to restock.

"Ok, well would either of you recognize either of these dialects?" asked Mialee. "This one is obviously Elvish, but the other two, I'm not certain."

"Druidic...and possibly Dwarfish," replied Shevette. "Where you looking to sell them?" as she looked to Samantha.

"No, we heard of teachings, would we be in the right place?" replied Samantha.

"I would be able to help you with Druidic...Mialee, Ayenna, or Saylinn could help you with any Elvish...you're on your own with the Dwarvish. Though, I'm sure there are a few around here that may be of help. May I ask where got these books?"

"Our grandmother, Elouise," replied Brick.

"Your grandmother?...Eloise? As in 'the El', Eloise?" asked Mialee.

"Yes. Well, these are my two brothers, and these are our two friends. Well, three friends. Simon here, has known our grandmother for some time and has been showing us around, beings how she is no longer with us." said Samantha.

"We are terribly sorry to hear that," said Mialee as she looks over to both Shevette and Ayenna. "We have heard so much about her. Her and Baba Olya spent many years traveling and questing. I wouldn't mind and I'm sure none of the girls would mind helping you learn, free of charge. It usually takes several years to become fluent in most languages. However, if you spend a few hours a day it may only take a few months or so to start picking things up. I would send you off with some sort of homework but I'm afraid that any of the magic or practices you wish to be using it for will be useless if you aren't clear and concise, you must be precise with your words."

Samantha says, "I'm not so sure that's gunna work out, we're still in school. Besides, it's quite a trip to travel every day, we would pretty much have to stay and live here with you for that to work out."

Mialee says, "Excellent, even better what do you say, girls?" as she looks over at Shevette and Ayenna. "I'm sorry, you don't look very excited" she said as she looks back at the kids to see them in disappointment, waiting for response.

"No, no. It's not that. Thank you, we just don't know how we would make that happen." Said Brick as he too sees the disappointment in everyone.

Simon agrees, "Yea, it's a nice gesture, thank you. I'm afraid I don't see how we would make that happen either."

Mialee says as she looks to the other girls, "Well...there might be some other way."

"Some other way?" asked Samantha.

"Yes, my dear." replied Mialee as she looks once more to Shevette and Ayenna, to see them both nod mildly, in approval for having already known what she is about to suggest."...There is another way, it's not something we do for everyone, but I'm sure Baba Olya would approve. We would have to conduct a ritual that would enable you to speak the language you desire, given that we use the appropriate ingredients. The gems used would then be put toward your staff and will be bound to you. *Soul bound*, if you will. That will provide the base most effective for elven magic, you will augment it as you discover your niche disciplines. It is normally a steep price, but we would be able to wave the cost of the ritual if you were to acquire the necessary ingredients...well?"

The kids take a moment to think before turning their heads toward Simon.

Simon says, "...lets-uhh, let's see what we are gunna have to wrangle up before we make any decisions here, okay?"

"Of course." Said Mialee, before walking over to grab a pen and paper. She waves her hand over several candles, lighting them to see in the drawer of the dimly lit desk in the back corner of the store. A couple of minutes later, she walks up to hand Simon the list. As Simon takes a look at the list, Mialee walks back over to the counter to take another look at the books that were brought in. She notices something after opening and exploring a little more of the Elven book that was brought in earlier. "By the way, this book is a cookbook...it appears to have a few handy housekeeping spells but it's mostly cooking. I would imagine there are more, right?" she said.

Brick replies, "Yes, a couple shelves full, we just brought a few to see if anyone could help us with them...there are all sorts."

Mialee says, "Ah, Okay. Well, I imagined there would be. Here a some of the symbols you will be looking for if you plan on taking up any elven magic. That is if you are still interested."

Simon begins to read off the list:

1 Golden Charm Bowl

1 Spool Shamans Twine

7 Bees Wax Candles

Elf Hair

1 Gal Aerden Spring Water

1 dozen Mystical Parrot Feathers

1 4 Leaf Clover

1 Yellow Primrose

1 Orange Vervain Root

Barking Willow Sap

Great Oak Sap

1 Howlite

1 Ebony

1 Agate

1 Blue Opal

Mialee says, "I'm sure one of the other girls wouldn't mind donating the necessary hair, right?" before glancing over at Ayenna. "We would normally be able to help you with a few of these items, but we have been running rather short on inventory lately. As you can see most of us have been out running on quests of our own. You could check with some of the other shops around but I'm afraid they have been experiencing the same. You also know that that this will only be for a single teaching. Those are the necessary ingredients per individual."

Samantha asks, "So only one of us would be able to learn?"

Mialee replies, "Yes, one person at a time at least. So, you will need to decide who will receiving this service...it is custom for the oldest of siblings to take on both the luxury and the responsibility of any given magical practice. You will have plenty of time to figure it out."

The two other sisters present pull Mialee aside to speak with her before she returns and asks to speak with Simon in private.

Mialee seemed mildly concerned when she asked Simon, "Did you plan on bringing these kids along with you to collect these ingredients?"

Simon replies, "To be honest, I'm still wondering how I'm going to find these parrots, or *Orange Vervain Root*, but yes, I was, why?"

Mialee says, "Aerden, Most of the ingredients from Aerden, less the gems. And aren't you aware the only place you can find *Barking Willow Sap* is Krueller's?...on the outskirts of the badlands."

"Aerden, that's Wood elf territory, right? Said Simon. It's beautiful, the kids would love it...And uh-no, I hadn't given that any thought, yet."

"Well, you should," Said Mialee. "It may be beautiful, but it is still dangerous, at least getting there can be...and yes, It's where I'm from."

Mialee makes her way back over toward the desk along with the Shevette and Ayenna. The kids talk for a minute before noticing an opportunity to speak with Simon as he is reviewing the list.

Samantha asks, "Well, what do you think, Simon?"

"I-uhh, I don't know about this one," Simon replied. "I might have some of these gems, I don't think the supplies will be too much trouble...but I'm just not sure about some these other ingredients, or whether or not you guys should go along for the ride. I'm sure we will figure something out though. Did you guys figure out who would be first?"

Samantha replies, "Ok, no worries. Sucks for you, Brick...ha-ha. He's the oldest, we figured he should go first."

Simon glances back at the list before saying, "Well, we don't exactly have a time constraint on any of this stuff. So, I'm sure sooner or later we can figure something out."

Raj says, "Yea, see. You'll be an elf, wizard, or whatever...eventually."

Moments later, Mialee walks up to the group and hands Simon a few rolled up papers.

Simon asks, "What is this for?"

Mialee replies, "A little something to aide your journey, it would be best if you kept that to yourselves. It would be a shame to spoil any secret routes, if there is such a thing anymore...You do plan on accepting this quest, don't you?

"Yea," Simon replied, "It's just gunna take some time for us to wrangle all this stuff up. I was just telling the kids I might actually have some of these gems laying around."

Mialee is excited to that and says, "Excellent, well I would have to recommend you stop by the *'Enchanted Gem'.* It is a Jeweler; they also do some gem enchantment. You can either pick them up now or have them set aside for you. They are pretty good about that."

Simon asks, "Next to the *Twin Sword*?"

"Yes." Replied Mialee, "I'm sorry to kick you guys out, but we have errands to run. It looks like we are all gunna have to do our part to restock if we wanna keep up with this shortage. I don't know why the sudden spike in demand is here. It's too bad you didn't get a chance to meet the rest of the girls, they will be so happy to meet you."

The gang says their goodbyes before heading back to *'The Beast & The Priest'* to check for their golden charm bowl.

The shopkeeper says, "Hello, again. Back for a lamp?"

Brick says, "No, we were wondering if you could help us with a *Golden Charm Bowl*, please?"

The shop keeper fumbles around though assorted botanical repertoire located in the back before returning with their requested item. They make a deal before continuing to the *'The Enchanted Gem, Gems & Enchantment'* and manage to get a couple of the needed gems set aside. The jeweler happily shares where they might find the others, only asking that they try and bring some extra back to stock, in return. They pick up Simon's bracers before returning downstairs to the bazaar to pick up a jug, containers, and new bags needed for their new quest before heading out.

Ch.7 Two-Blocks

Tuesday morning at Benson's house, about two weeks after their last trip out with Simon.

Jackie leaves in a hurry and says," Breakfast is in the microwave, gotta go!" About the same time Zack makes is making his way into the kitchen.

Zack, who is still waking up stops and says, Uh, okay...thanks." Before continuing over to the microwave.

Pete continues to skim through his paper as he says, "...Good morning," to Zack, just before Brick and Samantha find their way downstairs.

Samantha asks, "What was that? It sounded like somebody ran into the side of our house."

Pete says, "That was your mother, slamming the door behind her...she has job interview today, I think she's a little excited...Breakfast is in the microwave."

Pete sips his coffee and reads the morning paper, just as usual. The kids each grab their plates and sit down to eat. A minute or two of forks clanking and rustling from the newspaper before Pete stumbles across something worth bringing up.

"Hey-uhh, you guys were just on a fieldtrip at the museum the other day, right?" he said.

The kids are still waking up and eating, they all gesture with the same, "mhmm," at the same time.

Pete says, "Well, they just had a burglary...one of the exhibits is missing some things, some books, rocks, and old staff from a display...here, look." as he passes the paper around with a shot of the exhibit with the cabinets that had been broken into.

Zack says "It's kinda strange they didn't bother with any of the relics or old jewelry in the same cabinets."

The phone rings, Pete goes to answer, and a short conversation was held before sitting back at the table and saying. "Well, isn't that convenient? ...Power is out again, I won't be able to get anything done in the lab running with just the backup power, so I'm off for the day. I was just about to let you know I'll be needing the truck today."

About that time Zack and Samantha are finished eating and rinsing their dishes. Brick not far behind is the last of the kids to leave the kitchen. Jackie is told it may take a couple weeks or so for them to get through the other interviews and will be in touch regardless of news. Pete gets to thinking about finances and makes a comment before asking Brick a couple questions on his way out of the kitchen. Without realizing it, he showed a little concern.

"...Well, I won't mind the day off. I could use it. That's one nice thing about being salary, I guess...Hey-uh, Brick." He said.

Brick replies, "What's up?"

"Things still moving along well with work?

"Yea"

"You-uh, been able to put away a little money?"

"Yea"

"Okay, well alright, that's good. Keep saving...Have a nice day at school."

A couple days later, the kids are at school on their lunch break, discussing plans for the weekend. With their next trip with Simon scheduled for another week they decide to spend some time out at the pier that weekend. They run into Dr. Bromine, on what appears to be a date at the pier. Brick recognizes who he is with but can't quite remember from where.

They continue onto the arcade where they spend an hour or so before heading back out onto the pier, to grab snacks and talk. While walking and casually sharing with the birds something reminds Samantha to bring up Dr. Bromine. "Hey, did you make it through the rest of those tapes yet, Kate?" she asked.

"Yea, I think that was the last few that you gave to me, why?" replied Kate.

"I remember a Dr. Bromine in one of the interviews, I think it's *Patient 806*...the one where a young boy walks into the room...you remember?" said Samantha.

"The one where the subject starts talking in some strange language, like they were being possessed, right before they stopped the recording?" said Kate.

"Yea...that one." said Samantha.

"Sam, most of those recording have to be 50 years old, or more." Said Kate.

"Yea, there's no way that could be the same Dr. Bromine. Said Samantha.

Now at the end of the boardwalk, the group hangs out along the railing, staring out over the water. Zack agrees and goes on to remind them that the audio was pulled from pretty dated devices before bring something up himself. "What do you guys think about the magic stuff that keeps coming up?" he said.

Samantha replies, "Yeah, that it is kinda strange that different people are talking about similar stuff like that... Hey, why do you think Simon asked us to come back a in a couple weeks?...we were only there for a few minutes this last time we stopped by."

Brick says, "I don't know, he didn't seem bothered, just busy. I'm sure it's for good reason...besides, I'm still trying to figure out what we are gunna tell mom and dad to make it there over the summer...or what I'm gunna do about work, yet."

Samantha says, "Leave that to me...I don't about know those dumpsters though, I'm sure you'll figure something out. You should be more worried about bombing these finals we got coming up."

Raj says, "Yea, man...she's right. The whole summer is wrecked if you end up in summer school."

Zack says, "Well, you won't have to worry about not being home to move those dumpsters though."

The following Monday, Brick gets stopped by John while returning the dumpsters.

John says, "You ain't gunna believe it, kid. I just landed ya two more customers to your run, on this here block. The burger joint at the end of the block and the coffee shop right next door. I'm over there a couple times week, it's not long before us owners get to talkin', I Iett'em know how nice is not to have to be up early n' wrestle around with a bunch of dumpsters or have my employees do it, BOOM, now they want the same...after all, we work with food, not dumpsters, right?...What do ya say?

Brick replies, "Uhh-thank you...thanks, John."

"What's a matter?...you don't seem to excited" said John.

"...Sorry, I'm uhh, just thinking about my schedule, how I'm gunna schedule this is all." Said Brick.

"Alright, that a boy," Said John. "Already thinking about how your gunna make things happen. Okay, well, that's how ya gotta be. Heck, before ya know it, your gunna need help."

Brick replies, "...yea, tell me about it."

"I just did, kid. Hey look, I can even collect for ya, no tax, no nuthin'. That way you only deal with one person regularly, we're all business owners, everybody is busy. I mean you really should go introduce yourself and you know, stop by once in a while, since you'll be dealing mostly with me n' all." Said John.

"Okay, that would be great. Thanks, should I go now?" said Brick.

"You got time, right? Yeah, now is a good time. It's Mike and Jenny...Mike's burger joint, *The Cowbell* and Jenny's got the Coffee Shop, *Jenny's Joe*." Said John.

The next day the group is at lunch, just as they usually do. Brick lets everybody know that he has both good and bad news before filling them in on his talk with John and his new customers, courtesy of John.

Raj says, "...man, that is good and bad news."

Zack agrees and asks, "Yea, what are you gunna do over the summer?"

Brick replies, "I don't know yet...I think I'm the only sophomore with a car and a license, we don't exactly hang out with a ton of people."

Samantha says, "Yea, cus you got held back a year, and now you're stuck with us."

Kate says, "Uh, there is plenty of others here with a car and a license, besides my sister is in college, she can probably help us find somebody...just stay positive, focus on your finals. We'll figure it out, we have a few weeks before school is out anyway."

The group goes to work and begins throwing ideas around about who or how they can help Brick while he focuses on his finals. They start asking around and posting ads with Kate's house number, not to burden the Benson's, should calls be pouring in. A few days go by, no luck finding anybody, they remain optimistic and decide to head out to Simons that weekend with hopes that they will have a voicemail when they return.

Simon has them help out, starting with pulling out some old mining equipment along with other tools and supplies he has tucked away. They sit down in his den to take a break. He lets them know what he's been working on and begin on a game plan for their summer break, coming up in a few weeks. He rolls out the maps and notes that he has, he starts off with letting them know that he decided back to Bruiser's over the last couple weeks, and got to meet some of the other sisters, Baba Olya and Saylinn.

The two both expressed the same excitement and concerns about the kids. Olya shared a few stories and memories of Eloise. She also let him know that Eloise spoke highly of him and that she had no doubt that the kids are in good hands, noting that the kids are about the age her and El had met and began their adventures, with little aid.

However, she still wants to prepare him and the kids the best that she can for their travels.

Olya and several merchants and vendors at Bruisers had run with Eloise at some point or another over the years. She reached out to the those that had, once she received the news about 'El' and the kids. At one point in her rounds in Bruiser's, she got an idea to send off a care package to aide their journeys after the Priest had offered some herbs and ointments. The girls picked out useful potions and what not after she had returned. By the time Simon had returned, Olya and the girls had a rather hefty care package waiting along with a roll of notes with details.

The kids explain their situation at home and let Simon know that they have about 3 weeks to get things figured out on their end before they can commit to any trips lasting more than a weekend at a time. Simon had already figured it would be just that before they would before they would leave on any lengthy runs, a few weeks. He skimmed through the notes he was given and had begun working on a game plan to best prepare the kids before summer. He also wanted to go over the items along and the notes provided in their care package before sitting down and planning their trips out.

Simon began teaching them the basic navigation and survival skills that day that he hadn't already been taught before. Over the weekend, he also spent quite a bit of time focusing on setting up and breaking down their camp, so they get around efficiently. He had done most of the navigating, hunting, fishing and packing, before and wanted to make sure they kids could get back home themselves, should something happen to him. The weekend had passed, and the kids later went home.

Monday morning break, the gang meets up at school.

Kate says, "Well, we had a couple voicemails when I checked last night."

Samantha asks, "Sweet, is it somebody we know?"

Kate hesitates before replying, already anticipating an unfavorable response from the news,"...yea, both voice mails where from Louie."

"...Louie? Asks Brick as only one person comes to mind," The kid that lives around the corner from John and the other restaurants?

Kate replies, "Yup."

Brick says, "Isn't he, I don't know...TWELVE?"

Kate says, "Yea, we gotta find somebody else, I'm just saying that's all we got so far."

Raj says, "Wait a second, man. That kid is big...REALLY BIG...I heard about him."

Brick says, "He's TWELVE...wait, what did you hear, Raj?"

"Heard some kids used to tease him, used to poke him with sticks on his way home after school, trying to train him like an elephant. I guess he had enough, he threw one kid over a fence and punched another so hard he knocked the wind out of him...somebody heard it a couple blocks away. All of them took off crying." Said Raj.

Brick asks, "Is that why they call him 'Two-Blocks'?"

"Yea, man." Raj replied, "...Louie Two-Blocks."

Brick thinks for a moment before saying, "Alright. Well, there's gotta be somebody else, what did your sister say, Kate?

Kate replies, "Nothing...one, nobody wants to wake up that early during the summer. And two, nobody wants to move dumpsters. Don't worry, we got time. I'm sure something will come up."

Zack says, "Yea, we can always push our trips with Simon if we need.

A week goes by, and still with no luck finding anyone to help cover Brick's work over the summer. Louie had made more calls to Kate's asking for a chance to cover the spot. Brick manages to pass his Finals and avoid summer school. Now, the Thursday before the last week of school, Brick gets to talking with John about his situation.

"Well, kid." John went on to say, "That is quite a pickle, but I think this will be good for ya. This is your business and sooner or later your gunna run into these issues. Now, it's none of my business how you handle your business, okay?...But if I was you, I'd give that kid a chance. I remember what it was like bein' a kid and not being able to find work. All the paper routes were taken, lawns, windows and you name it was pretty much gone. Everybody was suckin' up all the gravy and I couldn't find nothin.'

'So, I took the savings from little odd jobs that I did have from helpin people move here and there to start renting an old hot dog cart. I couldn't afford a truck. Otherwise, I probably would have started a moving business, it was about the only thing left nobody really wanted to do. I rented the cart until I could buy one, I did the same with the second and ended up with about a dozen or so carts in my old neighborhood, where I grew up. I had to go through the same thing your goin through, back then. Somebody made me an offer for the whole business, I made some calls, ran some numbers and took what I got from selling that little business to get me in at this little deli right behind us, and so on." Said John.

Brick says, "Louie used to go around with a bucket and what not trying to wash cars...nobody really has him do it now that the coin-op is there."

"...see, that's what I mean," John said. "...sounds like the kids hungry...I got an idea, why don't you show him the ropes, see if he can do the job and you and I can watch from down the alley in the mornin and make sure he does a good job, that way you got some piece of mind and you go handle whatever else you gotta do."

"No way, John...I'll have to figure else something out," Said Brick.

"Ah-maybe your right...maybe things are a little different from when I was growin' up." John replied.

The visit to Simon's over the weekend went like the last, only Simon had some news of his own to share. He let the kids know that the sisters managed to find a few of the things needed to complete their quest, in the process of restocking. Some of which they had already acquired elsewhere. Simon was also informed that the *Orange Vervain* they will be needing will only by available through June, critters will have eaten all the flowers by then and they will have no way of finding the roots or telling them apart from all the other different colored Vervain.

The last week of school is spent mostly on finding somebody to cover for Brick. That Friday, Jackie gets a call to start work after the weekend. Pete is happy to hear the news and decides to head home a few minutes early to relax, being how it's Father's Day weekend. He starts having car trouble on his way home. The car is stuck in first gear and by the time he makes it home the car won't go into any gear.

Brick and Zack both head downstairs to help Pete out while Samantha brainstorms with Kate on the phone about Brick's work situation. About a half hour later, they figure it's most likely the clutch solenoids. Zack says he could probably fix it but wouldn't be able to guarantee anything, "I don't know, you might get 2 or 3 hours out of it, or you could get 2 or 3 years out of it. Let me see what our other options are." Zack said before calling out to the dealership and several auto shops.

A few short calls later, Zack says, "Well, there's only one shop I found that has the transmission in stock. Everyone else is over a week but our wait time for anyone to install will be about the same...the guy wants $1400 if he does it and $800 for just the transmission...cash only."

Pete takes a moment to think before responding, "...cash only?...we don't have it...I don't know if we could do it credit right now, even if he accepted it."

Brick goes into the house and upstairs to grab an old shoe box from his room. He comes back outside and hands it to his father.

"Son, there's almost a $1,000 here." Said Pete.

"Yea...Zack, call him back and see if we can pick it up, tonight." Said Brick.

Pete and the boys spend the better part of the weekend swapping the transmission. Sunday, Jackie takes the truck to the grocery store to pick up a few things, while they finish with the car. About that time, they get a surprise visit from Louie. Louie shows up on his bike with his game console wrapped up inside his backpack. He asked for a chance to work with Brick and said that if he let him down, he would give him both. Brick told him he would consider it and that none of that would be necessary should that happen.

Now out of school, the kids meet up with John, early Friday morning down the alley from John's Deli.

John says, "Well, good mornin, everybody...Hey, Brick. What happened?...You were swearin' up n' down, no way no how."

Jackie ran into Louie's mom at the grocery store about the same time Louie stopped by Sunday.

Brick replies, "His mom asked our mom to give him a chance. The kids he was having problems with said they were coming back with bigger sticks sooner or later. He wants to get into martial arts, they can't afford it. It's just her and Louie."

"Martial arts? Asked John, "Like-uh, Spruce Lee stuff?...or uh, what's his name?...Buck Norris?

Brick pauses for a moment before replying, "Uh-yea, John. Something like that. Shhh, here he comes."

John hands Brick his binoculars and says, "Ok, here. Use my noculars."

Brick looks to John with a confused look on his face and says, "You mean, binoculars?"

John replies, "No, why would I go BUY, noculars? I got a pair right here."

Again, Brick pauses process what process what John just said before saying, "...never mind, Shhh."

John finally quiets down but only for a moment to observe Louie before saying, "Look at'em...movin' it like it's nuthin'...that kid ain't just big, he's tall."

Brick says, "We know...shh."

"He should be playin' football." Said john.

Brick replies, "They won't let him play pop-worner, he's too big for his age."

Louie is now nearing the end of the alley way as John says, "Pass me them noculars, he's almost to the street."

Ch.8 Where did they go?

With less than a week before the season for their vervain is expected to be gone, they pack up and head to Simons. Simon sits down with them and goes over their checklist, to get everything in order to leave the following morning.

Two days later, they near Aerden, after their trek up a mountain top that overlooks the *Great Plains of Aerden*, they decide to set up camp and go over a game plan for the morning. They can now see the vast stretch of land they have to cover before the dense trees and mountains that make up Aerden fill up the horizon way off in the distance. Simon can already tell from the mountain top that nearly all the flowers have already passed or been eaten, due to the lack of colors scattered through the plains.

Simon points out to the low-lying areas that appear to make lines through the plains made from the rolling hills and says. "I think we should follow these areas through the hills, back and forth until we end up over there...it looks like that river runs right down the middle, we will try to set up camp somewhere along side."

Zack points to a mountain area and asks, "What's over there?"

Simon replies, "The opening of Aerden...the mountains off in the distance have an opening to the right of them, almost a horseshoe shape. There should be meadows at the opening that we probably will have the best chance of finding clovers or primrose."

That evening they set up camp on a little hilltop in the plains, alongside the river.

Simon says, "Well, there's a few red and purple flowers, a couple white and yellow left...but I don't see anything orange out here...we still have a lot of ground to cover though, so I guess that's good. Its gunna take us every bit of 2 days to cover all of this. Mialee said that the other side of Aerden is similar to this, but we will already be into July by then."

They sit around the campfire for a while and watch the horses go down to drink water. Simon decides to tell some stories and shed some light on a couple of other realms before getting to discuss the game plan for Krueller's.

Brick asks, "Krueller's?"

Simon replies, "...Krueller's Castle. The sisters drew us a map on how to get through the old road that leads to their, we won't have to go in. We just have to go far enough in to find a barking willow, get what we need, and get out. There should be a few on the old road, well before we get to Krueller's. It will take us a lot longer than before, but it will save us a trip through the badlands, where they can see us coming from miles.

Brick asks, "Why, what's so bad about Krueller?"

Simon replies, "You guys remember the petrified great oak?"

Brick asks, "...the necromancer den?"

"Yea, Krueller is a Dark Knight, his castle is home to them and quite a few others...a lot of necromancers, warlocks, witches...witch doctors, things of that nature...it's been a mecca for the dark for some time now...we shouldn't have to deal with any of them...we might run into wild boars, Kelk, maybe some coyotes on the old road...oh, and that reminds me, I'll have to show you guys a few things before we make that run." Said Simon.

They spend a couple days combing the plains before they run into a stream. It leads up near the meadows at the opening of Aerden's Valley. They spend a couple hours scanning the last of the plains and begin moving up the stream toward Aerden.

Simon says, "It doesn't look like we are gunna find the *Orange Vervain* guys, sorry...But that doesn't mean we can't pick up everything else we need while we're out here...Maby we'll have better luck next year."

The meadow is lush with grass and clovers, the group spends most of the day searching through it, before they begin to lose light and set up camp. The wind was blowing so that everywhere they looked nearly every appeared to have 4 leaves, until they got closer. They spot what they believe to be a mystic parrot, flying just overhead before going back toward the valley before they lose sight of it.

Simon says, "That's a good sign, hopefully we won't come back empty handed."

The opening to Aerden is filled with trees and several small streams that appear to join, filling to one as the rain fall picks up. Now lined up on horseback, they move alongside one stream, toward the town with Simon leading. A few minutes into their trip, they spot another horse in the meadow between breaks in the trees. Simon makes a comment before hearing one of their own horses make some noise. He disregards the noise, figuring that the horses are excited to see another horse and the kids are tired, maybe even a little disappointed so they don't feel like talking much. Again, the horses make a little more noise behind him along with a quick and heavy breeze that is felt pass across his shoulders.

Simon asks, "You guys that tired?...hungry?...you guys must be pretty bummed, huh?" before looking back at the kids, just to see the horses with nobody on them.

"...No...NO...No no no NO." He says as he starts to look left and right, back and forth for them. "Real funny guys...c'mon...jokes over, let's go. We're almost there."

With no signs of the kids, he starts talking to himself and the horses. "I know, I know guys, you tried to tell me...where did they go?" he said.

Daisy and Disco start to swing their heads and jump up and down. While Millie lets out a sad sigh before dropping her head and nodding in disappointment.

Simon says, "I don't get it, what do you mean?

Daisy and Disco both let loose a loud scream, then begin swinging their heads up and down before making a few more leaps into the air.

With a confused look on his face Simon asks, "...up?" before looking up, only to see widespread wings and large talons just before quickly being plucked right off of Bolt's back.

He screams and flails around in the air for a moment as they head toward a distant peak, Simon quickly tires and decide to go for the ride. He is now high enough to overlook a big portion of Aerden, what isn't blocked by massive Great Oak trees. Moments later he sees the kids on a cliff just below the peak they are soaring toward. It's not long before he is dropped on the cliffside with the kids and says. "Man, I'm glad to see you guys, you alright?"

The of the gang heard Simon from the cliffside and even though it was only briefly they don't plan on letting him live it down.

Brick replies, "Yea...are you? We heard you screaming the whole way here."

Simon says, "ha-ha, very funny. Did you get a look at who it was that snatched us up?"

Zack replies, "No, whoever it is, is moving pretty fast and has a hood on."

The whole group turns to the cliffside with a view of Aerden's grand network of bridges and staircases strung through the town with rope and large vines. The large bird circles around and heads back toward them, they can only see blonde hair floating around the hood of the rider as it nears. The big hawk lands, the rider jumps off, and throws back the hoodie before walking up to greet them.

All of them yell at the same time, "Mialee?!!?"

Mialee replies, "Did you know that you scream like a little girl?...the kids didn't even scream."

Simon says, "Yea, real funny...I noticed. By the way, what are we going to do about our horses?"

Mialee replies, "They'll be just fine, that was my horse you guys saw down there. I just threw my saddle behind a tree so you would think he was wild, works every time...Let me show you guys around."

Mialee brings them down to give them a tour of Aerden and begins introducing them to some of the locals. She also takes them to a shop that has the rest of the candles they will be needing before taking them to her uncles Inn.

Mialee says, "You can stay here as long as you'd like...did you have any luck out there in the plains?

"No, not really." Simon replied. "We just about ran out a real estate on the south side before we made are way up through the meadows.

Mialee says, "Oh, okay...any luck in the meadows?"

"No, we decided to make our way into to town after that, we will just have to get out here earlier next year." Said Simon.

"Hmm, okay." Said Mialee, "Well, let's eat and I'll take you guys to the springs before it gets too late. Bring your jug."

They make their way over to Mialee's, atop a very large great oak for dinner. Samantha falls from an opening along the last bridge they must clear before heading up a large staircase that spirals around the tip of the oak. Somebody below and not too far overhears the scream above. They quickly drew an arrow that was already fixed to a rope and fired it off to a nearby tree before swinging over to catch Samantha mid fall and swing over to a nearby deck. They thank the man and invite him to dinner, he declines and only asked that they be more careful, he was tired and wouldn't be awake should it happen again.

"I thought you fell, Simon." says Mialee at the dinner table, exaggerating a bit. "That's exactly how you sound."

Raj says, "I wasn't gunna say it, but-uh...I was thinking the same thing, man."

Simon looks around to everyone before saying, "...anybody else wanna kick me?...no?"

They spend some time eating, discussing things, and giving Simon a hard time before making their way over to the spring, up on a mountain. The hot spring has a view overlooking Aerden and a good portion of the valley it rests in. It is now dark and all the lights of

Aerden can be seen through a light fog that has settled in the valley below the star filled skies above.

Milee says, "I'll show you a spot we can draw sap from in the morning, before we go searching for anything else...did you guys spot any parrots?"

Simon replies, "Yea, I think we saw one on our way in,"

"Did you pay attention to where it went?" asked Mialee.

"No," replied Simon. "It was up over head. It flew into the opening of the mountains, where we entered the valley." Said Simon.

"Hm...okay." Said Mialee.

The next morning, they draw some sap and begin their search for clover and primrose. After the day is through, they all get together with Mialee's Uncle for. He is surprised to hear that she is looking for anything in their village, she should know where everything is or know who would have it, or its where it's abouts...with the exception of the parrots, they don't like to be found. He reminds her about a spot he used to take her as a little girl for the clover and suggests they visit a friend of his, a Dr. and Herbalist in town for anything else they may need.

The uncle says, "I'm a little disappointed you didn't come to me first, but I suppose it would have taken from your adventures and the time we got to spend here with each other...I barely see you anymore, Mialee...I'd also have to suggest you start early in the morning and watch from above. Maby you'll spot a few parrots, try not to hurt them...there aren't very many left. They like to use some of their own feathers in their nests, look for those."

Simon asks, "What happened to them?...if you don't mind me asking?"

"Outsiders used to come and poach them." The uncle replied, "None of them would go through the trouble of sparing the bird, mostly those using it to teach Tarvik, which has become the chosen language of the darker callings...they prefer to use a single tongue instead of a dozen feathers...they make me sick."

The next morning, they spend a few hours watching just after the sun rises for parrots. They notice a trend where some of them seem to be frequenting. A couple hours and several dive bombs later from the parrots and a few other birds that seem to be looking out for the parrots, they manage to pull the necessary feathers from a couple nests without disturbing them very much.

Not long after that they find themselves at a small waterfall, somewhere of the beaten path where Mialee's uncle told them to look for their clover. It was a matter of minutes before they found not just one, but two. They pay a visit to the herbalist who is more than happy to make the exchange for both the vervain and primrose for the other clover they found, now it is almost nightfall before they decide to call it a day and head back to the Inn. "Well?" said the uncle as they entered.

Simon says, "Just like you said, thanks...we left them nuts and seeds in their nests, they mellowed out quite a bit after that. We might actually have a few more friends now."

Brick says, "Yea, one followed us all the way to the waterfall you told us to go to and hung out with us there."

"Hmm...okay." The uncle says, "Well, thank you. That's good to know, I'll have to remember that. That's the way they used to be when I was a child...very friendly."

They have dinner, share stories, and play old games made of wood and leather that Mialee's uncle kept from when she was little. The next day Mialee makes an apology during breakfast before they begin their day.

Mialee says, "I'm very sorry if I wasted any of your time, my uncle is right, I should know exactly how to find everything here...a few years back I took a pretty hard hit from an allied golem that we had guarding our back, one that our team wizard had summoned to aid us. The warlocks we were up against had cast a corruption spell that turned it against us, they took brief control of it before our partner regained control of it. They took control just long enough for it to turn around and kick me. Olya, our cleric was quick to heal me, but my memory hasn't been the same since."

Simon says, "Well, don't-uhh...don't worry about it. You haven't wasted any of our time, you've been a lot of help, right guys?...Besides, we did get a bit more adventure out of it."

Brick agrees and says, "No, you didn't have to do any of this for us, thanks.

They thank the uncle and say goodbye before later parting ways from Mialee, somewhere on their journey back to Simon's. They spend some time at Simons before they had back home before the 4th, just in time for celebration.

Ch.9 Cool...What now?

A few days after the 4th, Brick decides to check up on Louie and have a talk with John. Louie is happy to have the work and has already started his classes. John says everything seems to be going fine and lets him know that he's been giving him sandwiches in the afternoons, before Louie goes to class since he must go by there anyhow.

Everyone decides to stay home for the weekend to hang out with their family and catch up on a little rest before their next trip out. The family gets to talking Sunday morning at the Benson's before Samantha makes her way down for breakfast.

Jackie asks, "Well, how's your camping trips been?...your sister said you guys have few trips lined up this summer...something about a new friend that knows of some fun new spots?"

Both Brick and Zack fumble for words before responding.

Zack says, "Uuhh-yea, it's been fun...kind of tiring though."

Jackie says, "I bet, I could hear all of you snoring the last few nights...she said something about mining too, that sounds like fun. What mines are around here? I didn't know there was much around here."

"...I don't know." replied Brick, "We didn't either. Our buddy was supposed to show us the next time we meet up." Said Brick.

"Oh, okay." Jackie says, "...you guys still hungry?...there's more on the stove, your sisters food is in the microwave." Said Jackie.

They talk for a few more minutes about Jackie's new job before she leaves the kitchen to get ready to go to the store with Pete, who is still at the table with Brick and Zack, sipping coffee after breakfast and reading the paper, just as usual.

Pete says, "Thanks again for the help with the car. Your mother and I went to dinner at the pier the other night and it didn't bog down like it used to on that hill we have to get over on the way over there."

Brick replies, "No problem...speaking of the pier, we ran into Ben the other day at the pier."

"Bennn?...Bromine? said Pete.

"Yea, Dr. Bromine, it looked like he was out on a date." Said Brick.

"Oh, well cool, good for him." Pete says, "Sorry, I thought you were talking about another Ben. We have another Ben working with us now, it's been confusing, we just call him Bromine now. I guess he jumped up on the other Ben's desk like he used to do with me, and it didn't go over so well."

Brick asks, "What?"

"Yea." Pete says, "He used to jump up on my desk or one nearby and go on these wild rants, he'd go on about sci-fi type technology n' all sorts of stuff...it was actually really funny...that or hurdling over things and screaming as he runs down the hallway like some rabid lab creature that had escaped...except the time he played opossum a few years back in the lab with the doors locked air evac system and alarm going, not all that funny. The only thing you could see through the lab window where his feet sprawled out from behind his desk...he had a respirator on the whole time...to this day I still don't know if he did it to be funny, prove a point, or have a two-person safety protocol put in place so I'd have to work with him on that project. We were the only two with clearances to do the work."

Moments later, Jackie heads back into the kitchen before taking off with Pete. Samantha heads down shortly after, as Brick and Zack are cleaning up the kitchen after breakfast. She says, "good morning," as she walks over to the microwave with her eyes still half open to pull her breakfast from the microwave. Both Brick and Zack turn their heads back, before looking back at each other and turning around, both saying "good morning," themselves as they recall the conversation with their mother from earlier. They watch Samantha walk over to the table to eat, both wondering how much she shared with mom.

Brick stops by to check on his customers. Jenny asked him to help move some things out of her store. Mike let Brick know that he had offered Louie work, helping his mother move back into the neighborhood. He let him know they could use another hand. also, that they wouldn't be needing Brick's truck, since he would be renting and driving one himself.

Both Brick and Louie help them move in and end up spending some time cleaning the rain gutters out and a couple other things before painting some things over the next few days. Zack, Raj, and some of Mike's friends end up joining by the second day.

Later that week the gang decides to head out to Simons. They notice something a little different when they arrive.

Brick says, "Hi, Simon... Hey, what happened to the trees you had on the side?

Simon replies, "What trees?"

"Exactly, they're gone...weren't there a few more trees?" said Brick.

"Oh...those trees." Simon replied, "Yea. Sorry, I—uhh, thought you guys would be back sooner. I got a little excited and had a little celebration on the 4th myself, I started playing with the Bows from your care package...come on, I'll show ya guys, wait til' you see these quivers." He said before gesturing toward the door to head outside.

Simon takes them outside to some other nearby trees, out along the lakeside.

"Check this one out," he said as he fires one off toward a branch. The arrow quickly turns into a Bola that slings tightly around the branch. "It's a *Bola Bow*, here, give it a shot." They each take turns testing out the bow before Simon pulls out the second bow.

"You ready?...Saylinn called this one a *Raiju Bow*...You can thank her for this one later. I don't know who to thank for the others," he said before firing an arrow at the trunk of the tree, the arrow strikes and immediately lets out a large cracking noise from the shock and splintering of the tree at point of impact. They take turns with that bow before moving on to the third Bow.

"...Ok. Come over here, this way a bit. I kinda like that tree." He says as he leads them up a way toward a different set of trees he feels better about shooting at. "If you like my bow your gunna love this one." he said as he moves them a little further to some trees that he's been wanting to clear out anyhow. He fires an arrow into the trunk from a good distance that explodes on impact, a good portion of the trunk gets blown out, the entire top drops, and falls over on its side. "Haha, it's a *Ka-boom Bow.* Here, shoot the ones next to it, I'm gunna cut the leftovers up and use it as firewood anyhow." Again, everyone takes turns before Simon shows them the quivers.

He grabs a quiver they had been shooting from and reaches into his back pocket for a pouch and sprinkles something into the carry pouch. "Give it a minute," he said before realizing he forget something, running over for his canteen and coming back to pour some in the same pouch, "how could I forget the water?" They wait a minute or two before noticing arrows slowly start to grow out of the quiver, replenishing it. "You feed it these seeds and some water, and they grow back," he said as he shakes the pouch and throws it over to Brick, "isn't that awesome? By the way I'm totally open for trade with whoever ends up with that last bow...just sayin."

They make their way into the house. Simon brings them into the den where they can sit around a table. He grabs a bag and pulls a few smaller bags out that clank and chatter like marbles when he sets them down, before pulling out a few other items.

Simon asks, "Which one of you has an arm?" The gang glances around at each other, not knowing what to say. "...Which one of you can throw?" he said after no response.

Kate says, "Mmm, Brick or Zack I'd say,"

"I don't like that answer" Said Simon," Who's got a sling shot?" followed by a show of hands going up. "Okay, good...bring them next time."

Raj realizes he is the only on without a hand up and says, "Hey, wait a second, man...I can throw." as he

Simon thinks for a moment before saying, "Okay. Well, we can figure that out later, I'm gunna hold on to these til' we figure out what they do, for sure. I thought there was a note for them...It must have blown away when I was playing around outside with them."

Simon opens the bag and pulls one of each color out into a bowl before going over them.

"We gotta be careful with these." he says, "I'm pretty sure the green is acid, purple is smoke, red explodes, blue freezes, and these 50/50 blue and red ones are fire...it should be from the 2 different dragon glands...we should also find a nice carry case or something for these, I might have an old garb belt we can use."

Simon slides the bowl over before reaching for a couple vials.

"Red are Healing Potions or *Heal Pots*," he says, "these are emergencies only, very hard to come by. Same with these, these Blue are Magic Stamina Potions or '*Mana Pots*'...you shouldn't be needing them anytime soon, but they are great to keep on hand. You never know who you might be running with that would need to use them, you guard these with your life...If they don't save your life, they may save somebody else's, possibly somebody who can save yours."

He pulls out what looks almost like a perfume bottle and sprays over the bowl he had slid to the side. The bowl slowly fades away, along with a portion of the table that was also sprayed.

"This stuff will only last a few minutes, its good in a pinch and I'm pretty sure it cloaks smell as well...there are some other things here too, but I have no idea what they do. Oh, and yes, all of this came in the same backpack, bows n' all. It will hold quite a bit, but it won't make anything lighter. So, keep that in mind...any questions?" said Simon.

Raj asks, "...can we test those marbles out?"

Simon replies, "I'd rather not, not here...besides, they won't grow back with those seeds and water...I already tried."

They help Simon pull some more mining equipment out and get things ready to leave the next morning. When they near what they believe to be the mining area, they notice some smaller structures along a rocky hillside. They get to the location and hop off their horses to look around, now a few hours before dark.

Zack says, "Looks like a little trolley system. I wonder where the carts are."

The rail system hugs the hillside before disappearing into the entrance of the mine shaft. Opposite of the tracks sits a small water tower and a few old wooden buildings. They don't see any recent trace of anybody and decide to explore them.

"Looks like a boiler room and generator." Brick says before asking, "You think we can get it going?"

Samantha replies, "Why?...we can just walk in."

Zack asks, "You really wanna carry all this stuff down?" before taking a look around and saying, "It looks like everything is still in good shape, we just need power."

They first check the water tower for water.

Zack says, "I can't believe it's still got water...we don't have any coal though."

They head back out to grab their things and start on foot. Kate spots something they didn't notice before.

She asks, "What is that conveyor for?" pointing to a conveyer.

The conveyer leads from a small hopper to the store house. They didn't notice that it sits behind another building they already looked at. No one bothered to check the other side of the boiler and generator system that had a hatch where it brought in the coal. After investigating the other building, they find their coal.

Brick says, "Whelp, found our coal...how we gunna get it over their without any power?"

Zack replies, "...dude, grab a cart."

They spend some time carting over coal before fiddling with the boiler system. It's not long before the generator house is filled with noise and smoke without any noticeable power being generated. Samantha is tired of waiting and believes that they already spent more than enough time on it.

Samantha says, "You said it should only take 20-30 minutes to warm up, it's been over an hour. You really wanna waste our lights here? When we can be mining...Just face it, Zack. You can't fix everything."

Moments later, now dark, Zack walks over and pulls a lever. The lights in the generator house flicker on.

Zack mocks Samantha and says, "*Just face it, Zack. You can't fix everything*...Let's go find our trolley."

Now that both the building area and the rail system leading into the mine opening are lit, they grab they're stuff and head in.

Zack says, "...See, now we don't have to waste any of our own lights."

Samantha quickly comments, "Wait until it runs out a coal."

"No, I made sure there is plenty, trust me." Said Zack.

Not too far into the mind shaft they discover their trolley with small box carts attached. They throw they're stuff in and begin they're descent into the mines where the grade down begins to increase. It's not long before Samantha makes another comment.

"This is slow and lame, we can walk faster than this." She said.

Zack replies, "It's not that slow. Besides, I told you it's not gunna be fast, just that it'll be better than carrying all our stuff."

A moment later, a large explosion echoes down from the top of the mineshaft opening, where they entered from.

"...what was that?" said Kate.

Zack replies, "I don't know." as the lights tremor and fade into darkness before he realizes what the explosion was from, "...crap, maybe that was too much coal."

They quickly fumble for their lights while the cart continues to roll down the tracks.

Samantha asks, "Why are we still rolling?!"

Zack replies, "We're on a grade and I don't know where the brake is."

Zack begins pulling the forward reverse back and forth, all the way back and forth with no effect on the cart before feeling around and pulling another lever. Not knowing it, he had pulled the release lever from the carts.

Zack says, "We're speeding up, whose got a light?!"

A few seconds later, Raj and Kate both get their lights going, just to see the posts lined along the mine shafts whizzing by and the sound of the wheels increase, as they continue to speed up.

Zack says, "Pass me the light!"

Kate reaches over to pass Zack a light, he finds the brake lever, but it doesn't seem to have any affect at that speed.

He gives it a few more good pulls before saying, "It's not stopping, we're gunna have to jump."

Samantha says, "Where going too fast, keep trying!"

He's unable to get the trolley stopped, both the trolley and two carts now separate and are rolling apart from each other. He says again, "It's stuck, it won't pull back anymore, we're gunna have to jump," as they enter an area of the mineshaft that levels out and opens up, just before the tracks split off in separate directions.

They start throwing their stuff out, accidentally hitting the lever that changes the direction of the tracks over sending them different directions. Zack manages to get the trolley stopped but the two other carts continue on their own paths, down the mine. The cart with

Simon, Samantha, and Kate head down one that makes a few long and winding turns before running out of track and skidding to a stop.

Brick and Raj's cart run down a track that also makes several long winding turns down before skidding into some rocks, and pitching them out of the cart. They feel around for their bag and get their lights going before they find themselves in something that resembles an old catacomb. It appears to be partially excavated, has stacks of tracks along the sides, and miscellaneous equipment scattered.

Zack grabs his light and begins calling down both tunnels, only getting a response from Simon, Samantha, and Kate. He can make out 3 different voices but can't make out what they are saying, he decides to head down the tunnel that Brick and Raj went down, calling out as he walks down.

Raj says, "This looks like a tomb, I thought this was supposed to be a mine." as they both have their attention fixed to one side of the tomb.

"...me too." said Brick just before they hear scuffing on the floor, followed by a slow rumbling groan that rolls through tomb from behind.

They both quickly turn around and begin scanning rapidly with their lights. A moment later a faint ghostly spirit mildly illuminates and lets out another slow groan.

Rajs says, "It's a ghost, man."

"Yea, it's just a ghost, it can't hurt us." Said Brick.

It begins to speak with authority while pointing back out toward the way that they had come from.

"I don't know it's trying to say, Brick."

"I don't know either, but it doesn't seem happy."

The spirit begins to get louder, continuing to groan and point in the same direction.

Raj says, "What does that even mean?! What do we do?"

"I don't know." Replied Brick, "Don't worry, it can't hurt us, it's just a ghost. I'm pretty sure it wants us to leave though."

The spirit reaches down and picks up a rock. It throws it at them, hitting an old metal bucket behind them before letting out a large groan, throwing its hands up and out to the side. A few more spirits illuminate to his left and right.

Raj says, "He just threw a rock, man. Let's go!"

Both took off running back up the way that they had come. They ran until Zack could hear the boys panting and the scuffling of rocks down the tunnel. Zack calls out and begins running down toward them. They both tell him not to come down, to head back instead. He heads down anyway to meet up with them before they begin heading back up to the way the way came.

The group meets back up where the tracks had split.

Simon asks, "You guys alright? what happened?"

Raj replies, "Ghosts! Angry ghosts, man!"

Simon says, "...Oh. Well, maybe that's why he said it was a ghost town."

Brick asks, "You knew there where ghosts?!"

Simon replies, "I didn't there where actual ghosts, I just thought he meant it was abandoned...ghosts won't hurt you though." Said Simon.

Brick says, "One started throwing rocks at us, we left before the rest did."

They make their way back out to the generator house where they find that boiler had exploded.

"Cool...What now?" said Samantha.

Simon replies, "We camp out here for the night and take off in the morning."

Ch.10 Tiger Rock

A few days later the kids make it back into town to pick up their sling shots and some swim clothes.

Jackie says, "Good morning, I thought you guys were going to be gone longer, everything okay?"

Brick replies, "Uhh, Yea. We forgot our swim stuff."

"Oh, okay." Jackie says, "Well, Louie stopped by the other day with a latter, he asked if we wanted to have our rain gutters checked out or cleaned, he also asked if you were around."

"I'll have to stop by before we head back out, thanks." Said Brick.

Louie lets Brick know that the last move job they did got him thinking about rain gutters. He also let him know that should be able to pay for his lessons no problem if things continue the way they are, and that Brick could have his route back at any time or share it. Brick does a follow up with his customers the next morning before everybody heads back to Simon's.

Simon says, "Okay. So, I think I found an old sword that might have one of the gems we're looking for. We may have to have it disenchanted, but that's no problem...I really don't wanna have to try for a conversion though."

Brick asks, "a what?"

"There's an Alchemy guy in the bazaar that does material conversions...it's pricey though...and dicey, there's no guarantee. The closer the material is already to what we want the better chance for success...you guys ready for our next lead?" said Simon.

The gang packs up and makes their way to the next location to search for gems. A few days later they find themselves overlooking massive, granite rocks, protruding from the mountains throw the lush green scape below, much of them blocky but rounded from the elements over time. The granite rocks have splits and cracks that run through them in a variety of different directions.

"he said, they call it *Tiger Rock,*" Simon says as he points out toward the massive granite slabs, layered, piled up, and clearly resembles a tiger the most. It looks like that's the one, across the way...there's supposed to be a ridge of smaller rocks that lead up like a tail, but we won't be able to see it through the trees. We should be able to find it once we get over there."

They head down the mountain along a large granite rock into the tree line, toward *Tiger Rock.* A couple of hours later they make it to the back side of *tiger rock* and find a rock with the mark that Simon was told to look for, one that will lead them into the cave they are looking for. It's not long before they find themselves between some of the massive granite rocks in darkness. The group pulls out their lights and continue inward through the damp granite. Before Simon can finish saying, "Be careful on the moss, it's slippery", Samantha slips. She starts to slide sideways, down the rock and into a crack where she falls a few feet down onto another slippery slab that leads off in another direction. She continues to slide before dropping another 50 feet or so off that rock and into a cavern below. Fortunately, the part of cavern she falls into has a large pool water. Her light gets turned off after it smacks the water.

The gang called out, "Sam!"

Kate called out, "Sam!, You okay?"

Samantha quickly surfaces in the water from the drop, in total darkness. She can now hear the gang calling out for her as she gasps for air and franticly tries to get her flashlight working, smacking it repeatedly.

"Yeah, I can hear you guys, but I don't know where I am. I fell into water. It's pitch black down here." She says.

Zack and Raj are up ahead slightly and notice a faint echo of Samantha's voice, coming from another direction and both begin calling out, "Sam! Can you hear us? Sam!"

Samantha replies, "Yea, down from the other side of the cavern, I think." as she continues smacking her light, trying to get it to work. Something rubs against her leg, and she lets out a loud scream. The gang calls out to see if she is okay.

"Yeah, something just rubbed against my leg though, my light won't turn on." She yells out.

They quickly determine it's a bad idea to try and slide down the way Samantha went down to retrieve her.

Brick says, "Keep talking, we are gunna follow your voice from over here. It sounds like there is another way down."

Samantha lets out another scream as she treads water, still trying to get her light going.

Simon asks, "What is it?"

"Looks like eyes! I see big glowing eyes swimming around, hurry up!" Samantha replied.

"We're on our way." Said Simon. "Just keep talking."

Samantha smacks her light a few more times before a couple more sets of eyes begin to glow and float around in the water.

"Hurry, there's more of them!" she yells out.

The group hurries down to the large crack that Samantha's voice is echoing from. A couple minutes later they make it to another opening between a few large slabs that run almost horizontal. Now with Samantha voice clear as day they begin searching with their lights. Samantha sees the light through a crack on the other side and begins swimming toward them, after calling out.

Kate says, "She's gotta be close, we have to get over this rock."

The boys give Kate a boost up over the rock before helping each other over, leaving Simon on the other side. Samantha nears Kate as the boys try to throw a rope back over to help Simon over.

Kate says, "Hurry, Sam! They're coming back toward you!"

The boys pull Simon up and over about the same time Samantha gets up to the rocks and climbs out of the water.

Kate asks, "Are you good?"

"Yea, I just don't know what's in the water." Samantha replied.

They shine their lights around the cave, unable to see whatever was in the water."

Simon says, "Turn off the lights really quick."

"What?" Kate asked.

"Just turn'em off really quick," replied Simon.

They turn the lights of and moments later the different pairs of lights begin to hover around in the water. Without hesitation Simon quickly dives in the water and grabs one before surfacing. The group panics and turns on their lights as Simon waves a Salamander in his hand.

"They're just, glowmanders." He said.

"What? Asked Samantha.

"Salamanders." Simon replied," ...they light up and swim in pairs with their mate...these are usually in Gloom Tide. I have no idea how they got here." Then lowered it back into the water, before crawling back out to pick up his stuff.

They glance around a notice little clusters of crystals on the ceiling of the cave, over the water.

Brick says, "Well, that's a good sign."

Simon says, "Yea, let's eat and keep looking," as he points to a lower opening in the back side of the cave, between a few stalactite pillars. "It looks like there might be another cave, through there. I can hear water dripping."

The gang sits around a lantern to snack and talk for a short while.

Brick asks, "Gloom Tide?...is that the place you wanted to take us to before we started our quest, Simon?

"Yea, that was our, I mean your grandmothers favorite realm...mine too." Simon replied, fumbling for a direct response. "I don't know that we will have time this summer, if things keep going this way. We'll just have to see how things go."

They wrap things up and crawl through an opening, into the adjacent cave.

"Wow, there's a lot more going on in here, I think this might be it.

The cave is littered with small clusters and have a few larger clusters, almost as large as they are.

"We should grab some of each, we can have them checked out later...we might be able to trade or use them for something else." Said Simon.

They gather some of each and try exploring a little more before calling off their search off.

Simon says, "Looks like most of these caverns have similar stuff, I think we found our tourmaline though."

The gang makes their way back to Bruiser's to pay a visit to the Jeweler. The Jeweler asks for some time to inspect and cut the gems down. They stop by the sisters and speak briefly with Shevette, before she closes shop. They discuss their plan for their run to Krueller's.

Ch.11 Son of a...

Days later, now in the badlands at *Paladin's Peak*. They can now get a better idea of their route with their map. Simon points off in the distance to the north where the mountains along the horizon lead up and intersect with more barren grounds to the left of the canyon where they would clearly be spotted from a far. Their map shows the canyon with several hills to navigate through that will provide coverage on the east. It leads to the old road their looking for. The road leads up to the canyon that they are told used to have a large bridge that spanned it. The road continues to the other side of the canyon, through more hills that lead up to Krueller's.

Simon says, "I don't see why we can't make it there before sundown...the girls said the best time to cross over is just before the sun sets...keep an eye out over head."

Hours later they venture down the rocky rolling hills, along a slightly worn path that they believe to be the correct trail. They decide to take a break and eat.

Kate asks, "What's that, Simon?"

"What's what?...where?" replied Simon.

Kate points up toward something flying up above and off in the distance and says, "That."

"I don't know...looks like a bird...it doesn't seem to see us here, so that's good." Simon replied.

The bird continues out a way before changing course and fading out from sight. The gang stretches out a bit before continuing. They make a short stop along the way to let the horses drink from an area that still had water from the recent rain. A few hours later, they spotted an opening between two large hills where the old road is clearly worn into the dirt. They proceed through to look down the road and find that most of the hills die out. The gang proceeds to the left, toward Krueller's and find that the bridge that was said to be down is intact.

They notice several ports dug out along the canyon wal, as well as a cave across the way.

Brick says, "Wow, I thought they said this bridge was down."

Simon says, "They did, It looks like it's back up...I don't know if we wanna take the horses across though. It looks like there's a trail down the canyon wall too, in case we need it."

With some time to spare before sundown, they head back between the openings to take another break and find a safe spot to leave the horses. They return to the canyon as the sun is setting and see some of the fireflies beginning to flock toward the great oak way off in the distance to their left. A subtle breeze washes through the canyon as they begin to cross the wood and rope strung bridge. A couple minutes of carefully creaking along the lightly swaying wood slats beneath them before they make it to the other side.

The top of *Krueller's Castle* could be seen from up above, where the crows fly. It's nestled in a valley that rests just on the other side of some large hills to their west.

Simon says, "Okay guys, remember the plan? no noise or lights, unless you absolutely have too...any questions?"

Brick replies, "How long did you say it takes the for the ointment to take affect before we can start drilling?"

"Not long. Maby 10 seconds...so, give it 20 to 30. Just to be safe." Said Simon.

"Then wait till sap is coming out before hammering the tap, right?" said Brick.

"Yup, this should be pretty quick." Said Simon.

They spray everything but the tools and bucket with their magic spray bottle before making their way around the first of several staggered foothills that make up the trail to Krueller's. A couple minutes later they spot a barking willow, just a way up the trail. Followed by a few more up a way, before the trail cuts up along the following foothill. The tools, bucket, and a mason jar of ointment can now be seen bobbing along toward the tree, with light scuffles from footsteps to match through the dirt and light brush.

Moments later, after bumping into each other a few times, the lid is off the mason jar as gang huddles around the trunk to apply the topical numbing agent. A very light cracking of the bark can be heard from the tree breathing, as it inhales and exhales through small holes tucked between the ridges of the roots. Seconds after the ointment is applied, the treetop lightly twitches before one branch reaches over to another and scratches itself, very quickly like a dog.

Had they not been invisible, they would be able to clearly see each other's eyes jolt wide open as the glance up, in complete shock. After some of the bark dust from above settles and a moment of the limbs lightly settling down as tree returns to sleep. Simon takes the brush as he nudges Brick, who is holding the old hand drill, signaling him to begin drilling. Brick drills a whole until the sap begins to weep out before swapping the drill for the tap and bucket. He firmly stuffs the tap in before hanging the bucket over the tap.

There is silent sigh of relief for everyone as they reluctantly watch the ruby sap weep out. Simon, who is kneeling, looks down and decides to reposition himself onto his other knee, at the foot of the tree. When he looks back up, he can see that Raj is no longer completely invisible. Moments later, a raven that had passed makes a strange squawk before circling back around and heading toward them. A faint red glow from the raven's eyes can be seen as it continues their way. It lets out a similar but louder squawk, followed by what sounds like a response from a few other ravens in the surrounding area.

"Uh-oh," Simon says lightly without realizing. He is positioned with the trunk to his left facing out, the opposite way of everyone else. It was followed by a conscious but subtle, "go" to the group.

Brick asks, "What?" as he also begins to visibly fade back to normal.

"observers" said Simon as quietly as he can. "The ravens are observers. You guys need to get out of here, now."

The ravens let out slightly different squawks, one after another, just before several loud boar squeals are heard off in the distance. A coyote then calls out with a large howl. The surrounding barking willows can be heard crackling as the limbs begin to erect slightly, from their sleeping position. They can be heard shaking quickly as they wake, before letting out a few howls themselves.

Zack asks, "Go where?"

Simon replies, "To the horses, I'll meet up with you guys."

A couple more coyotes can be heard off in the distance, barking and howling after the trees. The tree they are currently next to happens to be a heavy sleeper and is only now just waking up. It can be heard popping cracking while it begins to stretch out, as though it has bones of its own. It shakes before and letting out a loud howl from the vertical split between the bark just on the other side of them.

The trees are unable to see them but are more than able to smell and hear them when awake. The tree begins taking large whiffs of air through the rooted nostrils that can be felt at their feet as it begins to wake and realize something is nearby. Simon gestures, trying to signal them into leaving him behind, but they refuse.

Brick says, "What? No way, Simon."

"Alright then, I sure hope this is gunna be enough," said Simon as he pulls the bucket from off the tap. "Come on, let's get out of here."

Everyone now visible, begins to make their way toward the bridge. When Simon attempts to stand up and get moving he quickly stumbles and falls over, making noise with the bucket. He had earlier repositioned himself because his leg was falling asleep, his leg had fallen asleep because he placed the brush used for the ointment in his back pocket. Simon, who is still in reach of the tree, makes another attempt to stand up and get going. As he stands up, he feels up and down his side, feeling the brush in his back pocket and pulling it out.

Simon looks at the brush and realizes what he had done and says, "Aw-man."

The tree having heard the noise, is now awake and decides to take a wild swing at Simon, immediately after his realization. The group calls his name out to warn him as they watch. He is struck on the side of his shoulder, sending him flying and soon toppling down the hill side with the bucket handle still firmly gripped. All the noise provides direction for the wild boars and coyotes that can now be heard squealing and barking toward the group as they near.

Simon, now on his back, in a daze, takes a look into the bucket to see the sap slung all around the sides, but still there. "Son of a..." he mutters under breath as he shakes his head, gets up to look back, and see several boars making their way down the nearby hill side. "aw-hell, Gett'em!...before they get us!" he says looking around for his bow which is laying on the hill side, not far from him.

Like the ravens, both the boars and coyotes in pursuit have distinct glowing eyes, often red that show clear indication that they are under spell. This also means that whoever has them under spell can see through them and may very well be on their way too.

Brick and Zack ready their bows as the rest of the group hurries over to help Simon. Brick manages to snare two boars with the *Bola Bow,* sending them end over end and down the hill before laying down as they squeal. Zack is immediately dive bombed by ravens before he can get a shot off, but tries anyhow. One of the arrows strikes the ground by a boar, exploding and sending it into a nearby tree, knocking it unconscious. Another arrow strikes a tree, blowing one of the limbs off, somehow sending it into another boar and pinning it to the ground.

Meanwhile, the girls make their way down toward the bridge with Simon and Raj, as Raj fumbles around with marbles. He holds a few of them up to the moonlight to check them color and finds one he believes to be the purple smoke marble, to try and buy them some time. Unable to find his sling shot, he chucks it a rock on the hill side, setting the entire hillside on fire along with a boar. He had thrown a 50/50, a red and blue mixed marble that appeared purple.

The smoke from the fire wards the ravens off to a safe distance and Raj goes to pick up Simon's bow. Simon and the girls are waiting at the bridge for the boys who are making their way across.

"Zack, lemme see that bow." said Brick, "you guys go, while I'll cover.""

Simon says, "No, you guys go. Gimme the bow, please." as the kids take off down the bridge.

Off in the distance across the canyon is a silhouette of a horse that is seen running along the canyons edge, through the barren side just to the north of the old road. As Simon takes aim to fire off an arrow at a nearby coyote. One sneaks up from behind and begins chewing the rope of the bridge behind him. The silhouette of a horse off in the distance could be seen morphing into a cheetah like creature, now sprinting even quicker toward them.

Both Samantha and Kate spot a very large creature atop the hill that had been pushing boulders down next to the much smaller hooded and cloaked individual beside it. They begin yelling for Simon to cross, as Zack is nearly across and Brick more than halfway.

Simon looks back to the coyote on a nearby hillside, above the cave. He strikes the ground next to it, exploding and sending it into the canyon below. He quickly turns around and makes a run for the bridge, before it's torn down as boulders begin to drop from the hillside.

The nearby horse, now cheetah leaps into the canyon toward Simon and quickly turns into a bird.

As Simon sees that the savage coyotes are occupied with the ropes, in attempts to drop the bridge. He decides to cross the bridge when a boulder falls, smashing through part of the bridge right behind him. The rest of the gang is across, except for Brick, who to stopped nearly at the end to turn around for Simon. Simon, now free falling into the canyon after a failed attempt to grab any part of it, is now intercepted by the incoming bird. The catch is rather late in the fall, and due to the size of the bird it is only able to dampen the fall. Their combined trajectory is enough to send them tumbling into the canyon below.

Simon, again in a daze, rolls over to see the bird that had just saved him stand up. He watched it slowly morph into a humanoid with cat like eyes, both with sharp pink and green iris' that have a subtle glow from the moon and star light.

"...Shevette?" said Simon.

"...Better late than never, huh?" replied Shevette.

"Yea, thanks...I owe ya...you okay?" said Simon.

"No, this arm is broken and I'm pretty sure my shoulder is dislocated." Said Shevette.

"Looks like you have something sticking out of it." Said Simon.

Shevette pulls a bone fragment from something else on the canyon floor out of her arm before jamming it back into place by thrusting her shoulder into a nearby rock. The canyon below Krueller's is littered with bones and items from an assortment of incidents.

"...happens all the time." She said, as she rotated her arm back and forth, "I thought that was my bone for a second, where is everybody else?"

Simon replies, "Uhh, right up there, I hope." as he looks up at the bridge to see Brick climbing up the last few slats of the hanging bridge, with the rest of the gang waiting atop to help pull him up.

Simon and Shevette head up a trail that cuts up along the canyon wall near the bridge to meet up with the rest of the group. They decide to call it a night and camp out on the trail, mid-way to Paladin's peak. The gang didn't get to witness Shevette change forms before swooping down for Simon, they were unaware that she had the ability to do so.

Shevette says, "I thought you guys saw me for sure yesterday."

Kate asks, "That was you flying?"

"Yes," Shevette replies, "Something said one of us should be around just in case...I was in a deep meditation when I heard the first couple explosions go off. After I realized that, I made my way over once I snapped out of it...I had to change shape a couple times just to make it there in time."

Ch.12 What's a wand?

Now back at Bruiser's to speak with the jeweler.

Simon says, "You didn't say and about quality." to the jeweler.

"I know, I know." The jeweler replied, "...look, I'm very sorry about that. I get so busy that I forget that others don't always know what they should be looking for sometimes." Said the jeweler.

Simon asks, "Where does that put us?"

The jeweler replies, "Well, a lot of these I'll be able to use, somehow. But the ones here you'll need, haven't been the quality that you need, for what you're trying to do...I can pay you for them or credit you toward any service.

"...So, we have to go back? how will we know what to look for?" said Simon.

"Well, yes. I don't know of any other way. Again, I'm terribly sorry...I can make it up to you. Look, I know where lots of things are...I'm just very busy and to be honest I really don't care to go get them myself...I'm not the adventurous type and neither are my kids.

Both the son and daughter of the Jeweler can be seen behind the counter working on things of their own.

"...Right guys?" the Jeweler said as he looked back his kids, both nodding their head before returning their attention back to their own projects. "My daughter is into sewing and my son here has a thing for blades, they both stay pretty busy themselves."

Simon says, "Ooh, no...I've been down this road before...Every time I get ready to settle down and retire somebody talks me into some wild goose chase or adventure or something, I'm still hung up on the last one these gnomes talked me into, now I can't even find them."

"What gnomes? You mean those gnomes?" The jeweler said as he points toward the front of the shop door, where two gnomes passing had stopped for a moment to go over their list.

"Yea, those gnomes." said Simon, "Hold on a second." as he starts walking toward them, "Hey, I'v been looking everywhere for you guys."

The gnomes freeze up and look at each other as Simon walks up to them.

Simon says, "I wanna know what's going on, Sprocket?"

"Sorry Simon, we are very busy, didn't you get our mail?" replied Sprocket.

"No. Look, I'm tired of this run around. If you guys aren't gunna come check that thing out I want my deposit back, when will you guys be by?" said Simon.

"After this other one." the other gnome said.

Simon says, "...the other one? what other one? You said it was the only one you knew of like it."

Sprocket looks over at the other gnome and shakes his head before smacking the backside of the other's head, knocking his goggles off.

Simon says, "Oh, okay, I see...you guys found another and now your too busy playing with that one to get to mine, huh?"

Sprocket looks around to see if anyone is around before explaining to Simon.

"...We had one come in while we were another project, a customer asked if we could look at it, since we were already there...we should be able to learn from this one before we get work on yours...that's all I can tell you. Said Sprocket.

"How long before you get around to mine?" Said Simon.

Sprocket replies, "I don't know, sir. I can't tell you. If you change your mind after canceling, we have no choice but to put you in the back of the line."

"And how long is that?" asked Simon.

"I can't tell you that either, sir. Very busy, got to go, check the post." replied Sprocket.

Simon had a verbal agreement with the gnomes; the gnomes provide a unique transport service for many of their customers and clients. The service includes an off the grid move in secrecy to help protect the customer from theft. Along with an unscheduled inspection and assessment, which he is still waiting on. Simon doesn't recall being told that they will be in touch through the post in a way that will protect him, but it was discussed.

Simon says, "Yea, I know. Everything is top secret with you guys." he said as they take off.

Simon heads back in to speak with the jeweler. The rest of the gang is now behind the counter, now observing the jewelers kids and their projects. Simon is given better details on some of the gems and comes up with an alternative.

He says to the jeweler, "I have some old equipment laying around that may have what we are looking for, would you be able to do an extraction?"

"Of course...bring them in and I'll get right on it." Replied the Jeweler.

They stop by the post before heading back to Simons. A clerk flies over to help Simon.

The pixie clerk asks Simon, "How may I help you?"

"I'd like to check for mail, please." replied Simon.

"Name?" asked the clerk.

Simon goes on to spell it out. "Simon, S—-", and before he can finish with his name, the clerk takes off into the back room. She pulls his mail and returns with an envelope along with a wilted bouquet of flowers.

"Here ya go." She said.

Simon looks at the envelope.

To: Sigh Man

From: A Secret Admirer

With a confused but curious look on his face, he decides to open it up. He begins reading the letter and finds that it contains info from the gnomes; mostly details they already shared with him earlier. The letter starts to burn up in his hand before he can finish reading. He begins shaking it in a light panic, to put it out.

The clerk says, "Ohoo...a burning love letter? the clerk asked"...any idea who she is?"

"Uhh, no...I didn't get to finish reading it." replied Simon.

They leave to Simons and spend the rest of the evening combing through his inventory for items with specific gems. The following day, they head back to Bruiser's to visit the Jeweler and realize that things happen to be a lot busier than usual. He quotes them a few hours and informs them that the races will be held today and suggests they take his reserved spot while he works.

With some time to spare before the races they head to one of the restaurants and stop by a few shops along the way. One being, a *Pet & Ward Shop*, where they spend some time visiting with creatures, ranging from *Jackalopes* to *Water Elephants;* small, tusked creature no larger than a mouse but strong enough to attack elephants and consume their brains.

A waitress comes to help them as they are looking at the menu and provides the specials.

"Our specials for the day are Bison with *Sea Spider* or *Upland Trout*...comes with *'Cactus Cat Soup'* or a salad." She said.

Zack replies mildly curious and disgusted., "...*Sea Spider*?"

The waitress points over toward a large tank they had walked by when they entered, containing *Sea Spiders*.

Zack says, "I thought that was crab."

The waitress says, "It's very similar...it's one of my favorites. That and the *Water Leaper*"

Everyone but Zack settles on upland trout, he decides to give the *Sea Spider* a chance. Nearly finished with their meals, an assortment of instruments can be heard from outside.

"...sounds like they are about to start the races." Said the waitress.

They wrap things up and head off to their spot, up atop Bruiser's castle, where the Jeweler's reserved spot is. They have a great view overlooking a large portion of the peninsula where they take a seat. A large clock sounds at the hour and the crowds begin to burst with excitement. Moments afterward, the band begins to play. Once again, the crowd gets a little louder. The band plays a particular song that summons stone pillars and various obstacles from the water, along the outskirts of the peninsula that make up the course.

Soon after, the first set of racers take their place as the band finishes their song. Simon looked around and realizes that they have seats close to a set of cannons that are used to signal the start of the races.

Simon says, "Plug your ears."

Samantha replies, "What?"

"Plug your ears!" said Simon.

Seconds later the three cannons fire consecutively, the last cannon fires a ball that strikes a large bell that had been summoned along with the course, signaling the racers to go.

Bang, Bang, Bang, *BONG*, and the races are off, they spend a couple hours watching several different classes before the jeweler returns with bad news. He notifies them that one of the gems had cracked, during the extraction.

The jeweler had already pointed out the fracture before attempting the extraction. He also lets them know that he managed to get it to Aleks the alchemist, before he took off for the day.

The jeweler says, "He shouldn't have any problem mending the gem and will have it ready by morning...it's on me."

They return the next morning to meet up with Aleks and pick up the gem. While they are there, they take a look at some of his merchandise before heading off to see the girls.

Aleks' Alchemy & Allure shop consists of a variety of magical items, he personally crafts bait and decoy instruments, used for hunting.

Samantha asks about a wooden duck that is resting on the table. "What's this?"

Aleks replies, "It's called a *Sitting Duck*, when you put in water it comes to life; it only circles small area until you pull it back out.

Kate asks, "...And this?" pointing to an ornate box with mesh sides.

"A *Distress Box*, you put a piece of hair or something of that nature into the box and it will mimic distress calls of that person or creature." replied Aleks.

Brick picks up a gorgeous red lamp before asking, "how about this one?"

"That's a *Scarlet Lamp,* it will summon illusions; sometimes good, sometimes bad, it's used to lure, distract, or ward off an area.

They go over a few more items and make a purchase or two before they head off to see the girls. The girls are happy to hear that everything seems to be in order and decide that sometime the following week would be best for them to get together.

The gang pays another visit to the jeweler to pick up the left-over equipment and thank him once more before stopping by Simons and returning home for a few days.

Again, they spend some time catching up on sleep and with the family. Pete and Jackie have a double date with Bromine and his new friend, the night before they go back to Simons.

They pick up a few things from Simon's and head back to see the girls. A short while later they have everything prepared for the ritual.

Mialee says, "The instance will last as long as the resin last, unless it is interrupted."

The *Barking Willow Sap* and *Great Oak Sap* are combined to make a resin; to be burned and used as a heating element for the process.

Mialee asks, "You ready?"

Brick replies, "Yea, I guess."

The process begins and most of the gang decides to step out and give them some space. Not long after, Mialee begins to call out Bricks name. Brick is unaware the spiritual instance had already begun. He opens his eyes to see they are still there, sitting in the same room with Mialee sitting across from him, as if nothing had happened.

Mialee asks, "You good?".

Brick replies, "Yea...that was quick, is it finished?"

"No, my dear. We have only just begun. Is this location okay for you?" said Mialee.

"Yea, this is fine, why?" said Brick.

"Well, I can take you elsewhere to learn but we are bound to places where we have shared experiences, the instance is tied our mutual memories of locations. So, we can start here and move elsewhere if things begin to bore." Sais Mielee.

They spend several hours there at the shop going over material as Mialee teaches before she notices that Brick is having trouble concentrating. She asks for hand and in the blink of an eye their surroundings change entirely.

Now at Malee's Uncle's house, Mialee suggests that they break things up with board games and walks, in order to keep things interesting. With no need to eat or sleep in the instance, they spend a little over four weeks practicing and reciting, day and night. They also spend time exploring Aerden, sharing stories, and playing games in between learning sessions. Real time passed is only couple hours in the back room of the shop.

Again, in the blink of an eye they are back in the shop, where they had begun. The resin had burned out and their instance had expired.

Mialee says, "Looks like we are out of time, how do you feel, Brick?"

"I feel fine, thanks. You?" replied Brick.

"Fine as well, it sounds like you have caught on fairly quick." Said Mialee.

"What tells you that?" Brick asked as he thought about what just came out of his mouth. Without realizing it, he was speaking to Mialee in Elvish. He begins speaking normally immediately after. "Wow…okay, well do you think I will be able to read just as easily?"

"Did you remember to bring any of those books?" said Mialee.

"Yea, Sam should have them." Said Brick.

"Good, and yes, you should even be able write once you see characters again. Said Mialee.

They find the rest of the gang down the way from the shop and return to look at the books. Out of excitement, Brick is badgered with questions.

Brick asks, "Well, what was it like, Brick?

Raj asks "Yea, what is like, man?" before he respond the last few questions.

He paused to think about his experience.

"I don't remember much. I mean, I do but I don't. It's like I reached in the water for a shell. The water and most of the sand rinsed off, but I have the shell in my hand. I can speak elf, but don't remember a lot of the time spent there. How long were we in the instance, Mialee?"

"Maybe a month or so, I'd say." Replied Mialee.

Brick says, "…see, I remember couple things like skipping rocks and playing some games. A few bits and pieces like that."

Milee says, "As do I, do you recall what I said my uncle had asked of me?"

"No." replied Brick.

"He asked me to thank you for him. To thank all of you. For how you treated the parrots, how you left them nuts and seeds. He spread the word, they are becoming more and more what they used to be." Said Mialee.

A little more time is spent sharing their experience before they get to the books. Mialee combs through the books, she quickly notices one that is marked for elven shamanry, but it contains nothing of the sort. No one bothered to open any of the books after pulling them off the shelf.

Mialee thinks to herself as she scans through the book. She had always wondered how Eloise had navigated some of the locations as well as she did, and made a comment allowed before moving on to the other books.

"El would have one of these books...Whatever you do, don't lose this one. Were there anymore books of magic?" she said.

Samantha says, "Yea, there's shelves full, we only brought these.

Brick asks about classes, to get a better idea of what he would like to practice. The girls do their best to provide a description of some of the basic classes, such as wizards, clerics, shamans, bards, and alchemy.

Saylinn says, "You don't really strike me an alchemist."

Mialee says, "No, but El was a great shaman."

Shevette agrees and says, "Yes, but that doesn't mean a thing if he has no interest."

These comments go on for a few minutes as the girls try to narrow things down with Brick. Again, they go over a few more things about some of the classes before settling on wizardry.

Olya goes on to say, "Wizardry might suit you very well. Should you accel at this practice, you may even become a mage. Mages were developed by the elders for more confined and concentrated applications. Traditional wizards summoned golems and provided large scale support during battles. Mages were developed at a later time; they used similar magic to summon elementals and provide intense focused strikes for more nimble combat."

One of the girls suggests that Brick look into the book they had initially brought in, starting off with some of the more basic spells.

Mialee says, "It's time we choose your staff."

Brick is relieved to hear that and says, "Oh good, I thought you were going to say wand."

In a confused and curious tone Mialee asks, "Wand?"

Brick replies, "a magic wand, one you wave." as he gestures with his hand, as if he is waving one.

Again, Mialee asks, "a what? Girls, what's a wand?"

Shevette who had stepped aside to look at the books once more looks back and asks, "to wander?...why is somebody lost?"

Brick replies, "No, no I meant like the clerks at the bank or post use."

Mialee asks, "The fairies?".

"Yea" replied Brick.

Mialee pauses to think for a moment before saying, "I always thought those where tiny little scepters, why would you want to be like a fairy?"

Brick replies, "No, I just thought that's what you were supposed to use is all."

"Oh, okay... because we do carry scepters." Said Mialee.

It's not long before Brick finds a comfortable mahogany staff. They see the jeweler who helps with augmenting the gems. The gang picks up the staff and heads back to Simons where Brick begins his practice.

He begins with wizard spells that continue that gave him a difficult time before turning to the household spell book that he was advised to start with for practice. The gang got tired of watching him fail cast after cast and decided to go shoot targets while he gets his bearings. He recalls the few words of advice he was given on conviction and within a short while, he begins getting the hang of things. It's not long before Brick decides to look at some of the other books for the more exciting magic that everyone was looking forward too.

Over the course of a few days, he learns to summon a golem and basic arcane blasts. He begins referring to the golem as *"Big Guy,"* and the name sticks. He teaches him to throw rocks over the lake, to fire at with his newly found arcane blast abilities. The rest of gang uses this time to practice with their bows as well.

Ch.13 CZ47-X

"Good to see you guys," Jackie says at the kitchen table with the family gathered around, "Did you guys have any luck mining?"

Samantha replies, "Yea, I think we did okay."

Jackie asks, "You guys have any more trips planned?

Samantha replies, "We have one more spot our buddy wants to show us. How have things been here?"

"Oh, Good. School will be here before you know it...Well, you missed out on our date with Ben and his girlfriend, Sandra. "

"Oh, cool." Said Samantha, "How'd that go?"

"Nice to finally meet her. From what I gathered, she's an archeologist with a linguistics background. She has some interesting stories, traveling abroad. I forget what she said she's doing now." said Jackie.

Pete comments, "She's weird...I don't know what he sees in her."

Jackie says, "She is not, you should be happy for your friend."

"I am happy for him...I just don't know what he sees in her." Said Pete.

"Well, he seems very happy." Said Jackie.

"Yea, it's weird." Pete says, "Anyhow, I got to get going. Ben is supposed to have a presentation today, I'm supposed to help him out before. I guess he flopped on this last one, it didn't look good. It's not like him, it's very strange. I think the frequencies he using to charge and discharge this cubic zirconium are off."

Dr. Bromine had been working on a high capacity, high discharge crystal that goes by 'CZ47-X' or 'Dash X', in the lab. It has been the culprit for all the power failures and a number of other incidents in and out of the lab.

As Pete had suspected, some of the frequencies were off. They manage to get things back in order before his presentation that afternoon, and things go smoothly.

A couple days later, everyone is over at the Bensons for dinner, before heading out for a movie. The kids wrap up with dinner and head out. The power shuts off in the theatre about an hour into the movie. They are told that the power is out in the surrounding area and that they have no idea when it will return.

On their way out through the parking lot, they notice something flash off over head in the distance.

Kate asks, "What was that?"

Samantha replies, "I don't know. It almost looked like lightning...I don't hear any thunder though."

Sirens of a police car sound off a few blocks away and begin heading in the direction of the flash. A few more sirens can be heard off in the distance as the gang nears their truck in the parking lot. They hop in the truck and Brick turns the ignition key on without starting the truck, to tune into the local news. He manages to catch a live broadcast before it cuts to a commercial.

Brick says, "Sounds like something happened at the museum."

Zack asks, "You wanna check it out?"

A helicopter can be heard off in the distance as they think for a moment, before deciding to investigate. They head out of the parking lot and start heading toward the museum before they hear the news, now back from commercial. The news goes on to share that the museum is strangely missing several exhibits, nearly all the skeletal displays.

Another flash in the sky occurs on their way to the museum. The flash takes place off to the side where more cloud cover has taken place. Another helicopter can be seen searching near the flash site as the ground below flickers before the helicopter begins to circle the area and sirens fade off in that direction.

Zack says, "Looks like they are over by the Asylum."

Brick asks, "What's the news saying?"

"Nothing, they're still talking about the museum, quick turn down this way, I think I see something." replied Zack.

The gang nears the area they would normally park before heading into the Asylum and spot something hoping the fence. The Sirens have calmed down, but the two helicopters are still searching a nearby neighborhood.

Zack asks, "What was that?".

"I don't know." replied Brick. "Hey, look under that seat, there should be some radios."

They decide to split up, Brick and Raj take off on foot toward whatever it was that jumped the fence and into the Asylum. Kate drives with Samantha and Zack to the other side of the Asylum to watch for anything leaving.

Brick says, "Wait right here, Raj. I think I see something," as they near the edge of a building before saying over the radio, "Are you guys on the other side yet?"

Samantha radios back "Yea—", just as a loud screech followed by a crash is heard, a few blocks over. She glances backward for a moment, to see nothing going on. When she looks back, she notices something looking back at them. It stares for a couple seconds before walking behind a building. Both Samantha and Zack are in the back seat, taking inventory on the items they brought along.

Kate, who is still in the driver seat says, "Did you guys see that?"

Samantha asks, "See what?"

"I guess that's a no." replied Kate.

Zack asks, "What was it?'

Kate replies, "I don't know. It was standing up, it was staring at us, then it went behind the building over there."

Brick radios back, "Sam, you guys copy?"

Samantha replies, "What's up, Brick?"

"We found where the lights coming from...it looks like there's more than one."

Brick and Raj are now inside one of the buildings watching through boards in the windows. When one of the lights had flashed, they could see a couple beings that moved briefly across the doorway. "Looks like they are in the auditorium." Said Brick.

The auditorium flickers a couple more times before a yelling noise is heard, followed by some chairs crashing around.

Samantha says, "Well, there's something over here too." Over the radio.

"What do you mean something?" asked Brick.

Again, muffled yells spill from auditorium, just before the sound of the backdoor is heard jarring open. Soon after the door crashes open, several strange figures can be seen crossing between buildings, just over and to the rear of the auditorium.

Brick says, "Sam, You guys aren't going to believe this."

"What?" asked Samantha.

"The exhibits from the museum, are here." replied Brick.

"There being stored here?" asked Samantha.

"No, they are alive. We just saw some of them leave the back side of the auditorium, toward the lot in the back, with the house." Replied Brick.

The gang talks briefly about the possibility of them forgetting to close the access portal to the other realms behind them, since they were tired and in a bit of a hurry. In disbelief, they figure the more likely possibility is that someone else may have access.

Samantha says, "Well, Kate said she something strange earlier."

"Did you guys bring the backpack?" asked Brick.

"Yea, it looks like everything, but your staff, is here. Did you leave it at the house?" replied Samantha.

"No, I left it at Simon's." replied Brick.

"What is it doing there?" asked Samantha.

Brick was advised not to practice magic in his realm and figured it would be best to leave his staff at Simon's. Yet another flicker from behind the buildings down the way raises concern and interest. Before he can respond, the sound of a rear door opening echoes through the building they are watching from. Brick and Raj immediately head out the door and down and into another nearby building.

"Brick, Raj, you guys copy?" asked Samantha, after waiting sometime for a response.

"Yea, we had something in the building we were in." said Brick.

Some noise is heard just outside the building they are in, so Brick quickly turns the radio off. Raj points at a staircase that heads down below ground level, Brick nods his head, and they make their way downstairs.

Raj asks, "Now what, Brick?"

"I don't know. I really want to get a better look at what is going on out there." replied Brick.

"You mean the undead mob of museum exhibits on patrol? What else do you need to know, man? Said Raj

"No, there was somebody else with them. A person, I want to get a better look at them. This way heads toward the water tower. So, this way should take us over to the back house, right?" said Brick.

"It makes a couple turns first, but yea, it should." replied Raj.

"Ok, let's go." Said Brick.

Brick and Raj head through the passages toward the back house a way down before reaching back out to the rest of the gang over the radio.

"Can you guys here me?" said Brick.

Samantha replies, "What's up, Brick? What happened to you guys?"

"We cut the radio off to kill the noise. Look, we're in one of the tunnels, headed to the old backhouse. We're gunna see if we can figure out who is behind all this stuff, we'll get back to you guys in a few minutes." Said Brick.

Brick and Raj make their way into the old basement and office area under the house and go up into the house. When they look through the horizontal slots between the boards over the windows of the front of the house, they can see several of the exhibits and the backside of someone one, huddled in the small cemetery that sits just outside.

Light from in front of the person begins to shine through the huddled group for a few seconds, long enough to see several other creatures meandering about the courtyard. Thuds from below are heard moments before the newly undead begin to dig to the surface.

In awe, and still mildly blinded from the contrasting bright light, the two look back at each other. Speechless and only able to see the slight glimmer from moonlight reflecting in each other's eyes through the slot in the window for a moment, before returning their attention back to the courtyard.

Now looking back out, a cold wave of air seems to wash over and through them as they watch the silhouette of the person turn around and begin walking their direction. Their eyes widen up as they look back at each other before quickly heading back down into the basement, to enter back into the tunnels.

Brick is second to head down the latter, he drops into the basement and spends a moment trying to get his shirt uncaught before making it down. He immediately hides in the bathroom, behind the door that sits just feet from latter.

Raj had enough time to get behind the bookshelf entrance and left it with enough room for Brick to squeeze through. He also has enough visibility to see the back side of the basement where the desk and filing cabinets are.

Muttering can be heard through the chute as the person climbs down the latter and heads toward the desk. In a hurry, the person hastily searches the cabinets and desk. He scans the large, cluttered center drawer of the with his hands on his side before making a few remarks.

There is a brief pause before he spots what he is looking for. The silence is broken as he reaches down for a set of keys.

"Brick, Raj, you guys copy? What's up?" said Samantha over the radio.

Brick had accidentally turned his radio on, while getting down the latter to the basement. The radio can be heard loud and clear through the entire basement. He quickly turns it off and waits for a second.

Keys can be heard jingling as they're picked up just before a comment is made, followed by the drawer being slammed shut. Brick closes and locks the bathroom door as the person can be seen heading toward the bathroom. Raj loses sight of him, midway through the room but can now hear him twisting the bathroom doorknob and shouting.

Raj sneaks over to the desk and picks up a chair that he smashes over the head of the man before walking over to the bathroom and saying, "Open the door, man. I hit him with a chair, he's knocked out. Let's go."

Both take off running through the tunnels and make a couple unknown turns due to some noises, heard from the direction they were initially headed. They end up in an old storage room. It's filled mostly with old filing cabinets and miscellaneous supplies.

A moment is spent catching their breath with their backs to the wall, facing the door. Their hands are cupped over their flashlights so that there is just a faint glow, and enough stray beams of light to see each other.

They speak briefly of what just happened before reaching out to the rest of the gang.

Raj asks, "Dude, did you even see who that was before we left?"

"Uhh, yea I know. Dr. Bromine. Sorry, I'm having some flash backs right now. Did you notice something different about his voice?" said Brick.

"Yea, it was changing back and forth, why?" asked Raj.

Brick tries to jog Raj's memory by asking, "Remember, at the pier, when we ran into him on a date? at the pearl booth. What did his girlfriend do when that kid bumped into her, by accident?"

"Mmm, she flipped out for a second and yelled at him" replied Raj.

"Yelled what?" asked Brick.

"Watch where you're going, you little twerp?" said Raj.

"Yea...'you little twerp'...what did Bromine just yell, before he slammed that drawer?"

"You little twerps," replied Raj.

Brick says, "Exactly." before reaching out to the rest of the gang over the radio, "You guys' copy?"

Samantha, who is still with Zack and Kate replies, "What's up, Brick? Where are you guys?"

"I don't know, it looks like we are in an old storage room. I think it's just south of the water tower." Said Brick.

Zack asks, "Is it the one with the old fire extinguishers and phone equipment in the back?"

"No, it's mostly filing cabinets." replied Brick.

"Ok. I think I know where you're at." said Zack before passing the radio back to Samantha.

"Cool." Said Brick, "Hey, really quick, what was Bromine's girlfriends name?"

Samantha replies, "Uh, that's random, but ok. It's Sandra, why?"

"What did she say when that kid walked into her at the pier? Said Brick.

"She told to him to watch where he was going and called him a little twerp." replied Samantha.

Brick and Raj go over a couple things briefly before responding.

"Okay, Sam. I know this I going to sound strange, but I think you guys should check her place out, we have a feeling she's behind all this." Said Brick.

"What?" replied Samantha.

"Look, Zack says he's pretty sure he knows where we're at. Have him head toward us with the bag. You and Kate go check her place. Better yet, flag down one of the cops on your way over there just to be safe. We'll explain the rest later."

"Umm, okay. Sure." Samantha said before Zack grabs the radio to reply.

"You don't have to tell me twice, I'm on my way." He said before hopping out of the truck, pulling out a bow, and prepares to head their way.

Zack takes off in search of Brick and Raj while the girls start heading toward the helicopters, the figure that would be the quickest way to flag down an officer before heading to Sandra's shop.

It's not long before Zack must ward off a few undead on his way to a building he believes has access to a tunnel leading to the boys. He switches his choice of weapon over to something more suitable for the underground. Minutes later, a faint light could be seen through the bottom crack of the door, from down the tunnel.

Raj asks Brick, "Do you think that's him?" before they hear noise down the tunnel, from the storage room next to them. It was followed by a rattling of the door, from something trying to open it up. They hear something grown and something rattles the door again before groaning, "*Brains*," the voice quickly changes and says, "come on guys, open up."

"Yea, that's definitely him." Brick said as they both headed toward the door. Zack immediately started toward their door and is struck as the boys fling their door open and into him.

They return into the room to catch up on some of the details before going through the bag and preparing to head back out into the facility. Some noises echo through the tunnels that immediately change their game plan; leading them in the opposite direction they intended. They try to radio the girls, but they are out of range.

The girls manage to locate an officer that is parked, blocking a street not far from where one of the helicopters are scanning overhead. The officer isn't surprised with what the girls share with him, based on what he has heard and witnessed over the past few hours. He decides to go with them to investigate and notify dispatch of the asylum.

The boys find their way to ground level and are faced with undead before they notice some other strange creatures, and dealing with them soon after.

Raj says, "Okay, man. You had me with undead. Now, what are those?"

Brick replies, "I don't know, but they aren't from the museum. I wonder where they're coming from."

Zack says as he points off to their side, "My money is from over there," where a strange glow from a building top can be seen.

The glow subtly fades in and out as the source seems to expand and contract. It grows large enough and is close enough to the edge of the building, that it begins illuminating some of the floor below. Where more of the creatures begin to appear as they leap down from the building.

Meanwhile, Samantha and Kate arrive at Sandras shop, where they can clearly see that there is somebody there. The shop sign and front lights are off, but the back is still lit.

Kate says, "Looks like she's there, what do you think, Sam?"

"Yea, I'm pretty sure this is it." Replied Samantha, "Theres a back alley, pull up over there." as she points to a corner where they can speak with the officer. The girls offer to watch the rear exit from the back alley.

The officer says, "Okay, but don't make contact, just honk your horn if you see anything. All the units are busy and if you guys are right, we don't want her getting away."

The girls pull up through the alley, just in sight of the back doors, where there are a few lit windows along the side. Samantha opens the truck door to go look through a side window.

Kate asks, "Where are you going?" as Samantha quickly sneaks off down the side of the property to watch through one of the windows, while the officer proceeds to knock on the front door.

Samantha can see movement in the back area for a moment before heading toward to the front to check the door. Sandra spends enough time at the front for the officer to knock twice more before making her way back through the shop toward the back door. Samantha waves to Kate, Kate honks the horn.

Back at the asylum, the boys quickly run along a few buildings, to get to the other side of the building the creatures were coming from. They end up drawing more attention to themselves, after having to deal with a few creatures and undead.

Raj says, "They're coming down, man. We gotta get to higher ground."

"Raj is right." Zack said, as he points into the auditorium at a ladder that leads to the roof top. "That looks like our only option right now."

Now, at the opposite end of the building. Where the creatures are spilling from, they decide to make their way up to the rooftop. The ladder leads to a large, protruding, vaulted area. That side of the building provides some coverage for the boys where they can peek out and view Bromine, at the other end of the rooftop.

With their heads stacked above one another, they look from behind the vaulted area, to witness the light fade from the staff and portal as Bromine staggers off to the side a few feet before collapsing. The portal collapses soon after.

Zack says, "Dude, he just passed out."

Raj says, "The coast is clear, man. Go get the staff."

Brick grabs the staff as Zack and Raj go to help Bromine out. He quickly recognizes the n staff is from the museum once it's in his hands but not the large crystal it appears to have mounted atop; It's Dr. Bromine's CZ47-X.

Bromine is in a daze and isn't sure where he is, or what is going on, but clearly recognizes the boys. It takes him a minute to begin gaining some of his strength back and realize what is going on after speaking with the boys.

They try the girls on the radio and get a broken response.

Zack says, "Sounds like they are on their way back."

Brick says, "They are probably going to be pulling up by the water tower. Let's start heading that way."

They get the ground level and are immediately faced the a few monsters.

Raj says, "What are we going to do about all these? They're everywhere, man."

Brick can now fend them off with magic, along with the boys and their bows.

Bromine is surprised to see this, as they are trying to figure out what they are going to do about all the monsters and undead and says, "Brick, I didn't know—I mean, what, what kind of magic is that?"

"Elven, wizardry. But I don't know that much, these arcane blasts are pretty much it." replied Brick.

Bromine stops to think for a moment before saying, "Okay, let's head to the back house. I might have something there we could use."

They catch a break for a moment and make it a few buildings up toward the back house, where they are faced again with a variety of creatures and undead. Overwhelmed with what is off in the distance, Brick decides to summon a golem to help them continue.

Brick stops and says, "Hold up." and begins summoning.

Raj asks, "Hold up? For what? Let's go, man!"

"Just cover me for a minute, look what's on its way." replied Brick, pointing to an incoming mob of monsters.

Now near the cemetery, opposite end of the back house, Brick begins to summon a golem from the surrounding earth. It takes him about a minute to do so. The earthy companion containing dirt, rocks and even nearby tombstones begins pummeling monsters as they get swarmed. It's not long before they get things under control and feel comfortable enough to head down into the basement of the house and leave the golem to watch outside.

Bromine says, "Here, Brick. Look in that drawer over there, see if there is anything you recognize."

"What?" asked Brick.

"You said, elven, right?" asked Bromine.

"Yea." replied Brick.

Bromine opens the drawer and continues to explain, "My dad used to keep all sorts of papers that patients would write down. Stuff that they claimed to be magic. Maby some of it's real. If any of it is, hopefully it's Elven." He said.

Both Brick and Bromine begin going through the drawers and cabinets. Bromine begins to lay anything on the desk that isn't in English, including drawings. Moments later, Bromine finishes up with the cabinets as Brick is scanning through papers on the desk. Brick finds a few papers with elven characters and writing but nothing that resembles magic. At least from what he has seen, they're mostly thoughts and remarks.

Zack grabs a hand full of papers tucked away on a shelf with strange characters and says, "Dude, what are these?"

"Well, I don't know what these are, but I can tell you what this is." Brick said, as he starts scanning through a book from the same shelf with elven characters plain as day on the spine. "Looks like a cleric's book." He said.

Bromine asks, "Cleric?"

"Yea, elven cleric magic." Replied Brick, "We have one at Simons, but I haven't spent much time with it."

Soon after, the girls reach out over the radio.

Samantha says, "We are out by the water tower, on the north end. Where are you guys?"

Brick replies, "The back house, with Dr. Bromine. We think we found something that might help us. How are things looking out there?" as Raj notices a change in the noise coming from outside. The pummeling had slowed and so he heads up to check on things.

In the meantime, Brick continues to discuss things for a few moments with the girls.

Raj returns to the basement with news, "Looks like most of those creatures are done, man."

Brick says, "Sam said, the other creatures turned and headed back our way, once they heard what was going on, but the undead where still roaming."

Raj says, "Well, it looks like the golem got them, so now we just have to figure out what to do about the undead. You find anything that will do us some good?"

Brick replies, "Other than, buffs and heals? Yea, I think one of these two spells right here, will work. It's between *Night Fog* and *Cloudburst*. It says here, either will work for undead."

Zack asks, "Which is quicker?"

"It looks like, *Night Fog* it is. Besides, it recommends that we be on higher ground for *Cloudburst*." Replied Brick.

"Okay, let's give it a shot." Said Zack.

The gang now heads out into the courtyard, alongside the Golem, and Brick begins casting the *Night Fog* spell. Moments later, a low-lying fog begins to rise in the immediate area, and slowly fills the courtyard. Bones from the undead can be heard off in the distance, dropping to the ground, as if someone had just slid piles of them from off a countertop.

Samantha asks, "Where are you guys? It's getting foggy out here."

Raj grabs the radio to respond, while Brick continues casting, pushing the fog out as far he can, before taking a break.

Raj says, "That's us. Well, it's Brick. The undead should be dropping like flies now. How far out is the fog?"

Samantha replies, "I'd say out passed the monument, by the signal."

They make their way to the girls and quickly jump into the truck.

Kate asks, "So, what's the game plan?"

Brick replies, "I don't know, it looks like they still have their hands full, pull over there." as he points toward a helicopter off in the distance.

The gang encounters a few undead along the way to a foothill where they believe Brick will be best positioned to cast Cloudburst spell. Clouds begin to fill the air, remaining undead in town begin to fall apart, slowly collapsing from the dispelling rainfall.

Ch.14 What are these?

Days later at Simon's, after the town had been saved. They get ready for Gloom Tide. With just a couple of weeks before school, the gang decides to invite Bromine.

Simon says, "Glad, you guys could make it. I didn't think you guys were coming," He had put all the gear back away after a few days had passed from when they said they would be there. "Here, put this in your bag," he adds, as he passes a bottle with a dropper top to Samantha, sitting next to their backpack.

Samantha says, "Uh-sure, what's this?" as she places the bottle in their bag.

"A little something to add to your bag of tricks. You'll see when we get to Gloom Tide." replied Simon.

A day and half later, they find themselves in a humid cave with water flowing at their feet. The cavern is dimly lit by various veins of rock grain that run through the cave. The veins can be seen below water, running along the stream walls, along with a several glowing fish varying in color drift along.

Brick Reads the dropper bottle that Simon had given them, "two-four, hr, fish...Hm, this seems like a small bottle for 24 fish, even for girl fish."

Samantha says, "Let me see that. That's 24 hours, Brick."

"Yes, that's 24-hour gills. I have my own bottle, that one is for you guys. It's 24 hours from the last drop. One drop will do, give it few seconds. Oh, and pay attention to the time." Said Simon.

A few moments and laughs later, the gang heads down into the water. They follow Simon down a way before the natural current begins to carry them off. The channel still contains various patches and rock grains that glow, along with a variety of bright sea life. They drift through what looks like black lit aquarium until Simon surfaces.

Simon says with excitement, "Ah-Ha, it's still there," looking at a boat he had left tide up, some time ago, in a jetty just off the channel."

He heads toward the boat, everyone else is still struck by the view of the surface. They crawl up some scattered opaque rocks that run along the channel and stare out at the abundance of stars that fill the sky with an assortment of trees, and wildlife. Nearly everything has a nightly characteristic that glows, even the trees seem to trickle with light.

Simon says, "Come on, help me push this boat out. We don't want to be late for breakfast."

Samantha asks, "You mean, Dinner?"

"No, it's always night on this side of the planet. The internal temp keeps this side nice and warm."

Some time is spent navigating through the warm tropics before arriving at the village. The gang ties the boat up and heads up more opaque rocks, all sorts, deep in color. They run along a creek, like massive hunks of worn-down acrylic that lead into the trees, just outside the village.

Raj, who is off to the side, staring at a tree asks, "What are these?"

"The bugs?" Simon asked, having noticed bugs around the tree that Raj is staring at.

"No," replied to Raj, "Hanging from the tree." He said with his eye's laser focused.

"Oh, they're fruit. Are you that hungry? We are almost there." Said Simon.

"...ok." Raj said as the gleam in his eye wilted.

After noticing the immediate disappointment Simon says, "Go ahead and grab some, we will bring some up for everybody."

They continue up the creek after collecting some fruit, only to be snared by a large net along the creek side. Several large stone defense totems rise from all around before Simon yells out, "Don't shoot, Don't Shoot. Jabadak, is that you?"

There is a brief pause before a voice responds, "No, this is Verrnak, his sister. Who are you?"

Verrnak is a Humanoid Frog, an *Amphibilock*, belonging to one of several amphibious and reptile-based tribes in *Gloom Tide*.

"It's Simon, and some friends." replied Simon.

With no response, the snare is lowered, and the totem pillars recede back into the ground.

"Hi, Simon. Why would you think this was Jaba? He doesn't know how to summon totems." Said Verrnak.

"Oh, I don't know, the last two times this happened, he was here...But so were you. Where is Jabadak?" replied Simon.

"Out with some *Merlocks*, somewhere in the *Sunken Hollows*." Verrnak said, referring to a type of mermaid from a nearby realm. "I don't know when he will be back."

"Okay. Well, we brought up some fruit." Simon said, before introducing everyone else. Not long after breakfast, they find themselves hiking up to some hot springs where they spend the remainder of the day.

The following day, Verrnak takes them to a fishing spot, where Jabadak later finds them. He decides to sneak up on them from behind, after tying their fishing line to a log.

Jabadak asks, "So, what brings you guys to *Gloom Tide*?"

Simon replies, "It's our last trip before the kids go back to school. Oh, and I wanted to get your gloves back to you."

"I put them on your bed, Jaba." said Verrnak.

Jabadak asks, "How long before you head out, Simon?"

"We really should head back in a few days." replied Simon.

"Hope you brought your gills." Said Jabadak.

The next few days are spent with Jabadak, exploring *Gloom Tide* before heading back to Simons. They make a stop at Bruiser's on their way back, where they pay a visit to the girls.

They share their experiences had at home before they made their trip to *Gloom Tide* and go on to discuss a few other things.

Olya says, "Glad to hear things went well. Have you given any thought as to who would be next?"

Brick asks, "Next?"

"Yes, Next." Replied Olya, "You have given it some thought, no?"

Brick looks around to the gang as he says, "Well, Sam and Zack are both the same age, soo."

Simon is pretty worn out from the trip, "Woah-woah-woah, don't you think it's a little soon for this? You guys will back in school next week." He says.

Olya replies, "No, not at all. I'm not suggesting they start their quest now. I'm only curious, as to whether they have given it the thought."

Zack says, "I'm not so sure I want to take up magic, what about you, Sam?"

"Well, Yea...of course I'd like to." replied Samantha.

Olya asks, "And have you given any thought to what you'd like to learn?"

Samantha replies, "Shamanry sounds like something I could get into, I'll be able to summon attack pillars and heal, right?"

"They are called totems, but yes. Along with a number of other things. And you my dear?" said Olya, now looking to Kate.

"Me? Uh, well... a Cleric." replied Kate.

"Ah, I see. You two, like your grandmother and I?" said Olya, "and you?" now looking to Raj.

"I wouldn't mind being able to turn into different animals." replied Raj, "So maybe a druid, like Shevette."

Olya says, "Shevette, you hear that?"

"I sure do, let's hope your spirit type will allow it." replied Shevette.

Olya says, "Yes, lets. Well, that's good. That's all I hoped any one of you would have to say. It is nice to hear interest. It is okay if you don't."

Raj asks, "Yea, what's up with that, man? You really don't want to learn anything? You'll probably pick up on things a lot of this faster than all of us."

Zack replies, "I didn't say I didn't want to learn anything. I just don't know about magic. Something about training with the monks sounds more interesting, more my style."

Simon asks, "Even after everything I've told you, kid?...You still want to give that a go?"

"Yea, I do" replied Zack, "You knew, you gave it a shot. It didn't work out and you had enough respect to leave it be, right? You gave it a shot, it's not like you quit before you started. I can always take up magic if doesn't work out."

Simon says, "Well, maybe after the gnomes get around to fixing that craft. We'll need it to get to *the Nexus,* for the *Odd Realms…*that's where you find the Monks.. It'll be a lot better than paying for a lift there."

The gang spends a little more time discussing who might be up next before heading back home where speak with Bromine for a bit. He had been very quiet due to being overwhelmed with both old memories, and new ideas throughout most of their trip.

He goes on to say, "I wanted to thank you guys for bringing me along with you, It really was a lot to take in."

Brick says, "No problem, we figured if anybody would appreciate it, it would be you. You were pretty quiet though...are you good?"

Bromine replies, "Yea, It's just unbelievable, everything I grew up wondering and more, is real. I can't help but try to figure out how, or try to understand how, is all.

The gang returns home to catch up on rest before the start of school. Bromine returns to work with projects in mind and Simon takes another look through his inventory, after catching up on some well needed rest of course.

The End.